BRIDGES OF STARLIGHT

Dana Tanaro Britt

Cover Design by Emily Clanton
Edited by Sophie Weeks

This is a work of fiction. Names, characters, places, brands, media, and incidents are either the product of the author's imagination or are used fictitiously. Any resemblance to similarly named places or to persons living or deceased is unintentional.

To That Husband o' Mine, my Hero, my Anchor, my Number One--
thank you for making my dreams come true, over and over again.

CHAPTER ONE

"OWEN FORD CALLAHAN, so help me Baby Jesus, if I trip over another animal, you're all going to the zoo—every last one of you!" Katie shrieked as a lizard ran across one bare foot and a puppy promptly peed on the other.

The two little girls sprawled on the floor of the room coloring giggled at their mother hopping around as she tried to avoid stepping on both the puddle and the puppy. Katie glared at them, biting her lip against a grin. "Just in case you didn't catch it, that means the both of you, too!" Her pseudo-stern admonishment brought about more giggles compounded by the exuberant puppy happily licking faces and barking.

"Sorry, Mom, I was about to take Scout out when Sizzle got escaped from his cage." The mop-topped owner of the pet menagerie ran in the back door, lizard triumphantly in hand.

Katie again tried for a stern affect, giving up when the almost ten-year-old grinned at her with an exact replica of his father's mischievous expression. Shaking her head, she merely handed him a towel from the laundry spilling out of the basket she'd dropped in the chaos.

"I'll put Sizzle up for you." Seven-year-old Miri took the wriggling lizard and ran off to the back of the house, followed closely by her three-year-old sister.

"At least it's not carpet, right, Mom?" Owen cleaned up the puppy's mess and dashed back out the door with said puppy at his heels. "C'mon, Scout!"

"It's good to see that some things never change." The voice from her dreams froze Katie in her tracks. Whirling around, she dropped the laundry basket she'd just picked up.

Ford winced as the basket narrowly missed her foot. "Those feet—you're always either stepping on something or dropping something on them."

Katie ignored the basket and the comment, her breath gone, her eyes devouring the man leaning heavily against the door frame. Dear God, he looked exhausted yet wonderful. His dark hair was a bit longer than the Army usually liked, an olive green t-shirt stretching across the broad chest she'd clung to so many times—he'd lost weight, but seemed bigger at the same time. It took all she had to hold on to her deep-seated anger and not run to throw her arms around him.

"I thought you'd call or email before showing up," Katie said sharply, cringing a little inside when his expression went blank at her harsh tone.

"I thought I would, too." He shrugged.

The house erupted with shrieks and screams as Miri rounded the corner and saw him.

"Oh. My. Stars. It's Daddy! Daddy! Daddy! Daddy!" Flinging her body at her father, the girl nearly took him down before he could brace himself. Ford swung her up, her arms tightly around his neck in seconds. "I missed you so, so, so much, Daddy!"

"Whoa! Hey, Dad!" Owen flew across the room and flung his arms around Ford's torso, burying his face in his father's side.

Thankfully, Katie was still tuned into her husband and still thought enough of him to step in when he staggered just a little under the onslaught. "Hey, kiddos, let's let Daddy sit down, okay? He's had an even longer trip than we did to get here." The squint to his eyes and tightness to his jaw had her on alert.

"Really? Cause it took us for-ever!" Miri's eyes were wide as she led him to the couch and sat on the arm next to him.

Owen scoffed at his sister, "If it took forever, he wouldn't be here now, silly."

Ford chuckled and tousled his son's wavy hair. "All secure?" he asked the boy, gaze intent on slate blue eyes that mirrored his own. This was how he asked about things each time they talked while he was away and when he returned, giving the boy purpose as man of the house in a world where his father was away.

Owen nodded, grinning proudly. "All secure."

Still standing in the middle of the room, Katie watched the man she'd loved for over ten years, the man she was furious with, the man whose house she'd packed up while he was away, as he reconnected with their children. She watched him tilt his head and smile at his youngest child, whose body she could feel leaning against the back of her legs. He patted the couch next to him, entreating her to come closer. Scarlett shook her head, but did inch over to stand next to her sister.

While Katie's anger and hurt would not be easily dismissed and she hadn't expected him to just show up, she *was* glad he was safe and glad he was here. The kids needed their daddy.

She, however, wasn't going to need him—or anyone—ever again.

* * *

In the bathroom, Ford scooped cold water into his hands and splashed his face several times, lingering on the last splash to press his fingers to his eyes. His head pounded, tender with residual pain, travel fatigue and the bedlam that came with a household of hyped up children and various critters. If his head didn't explode first, he thought his heart might burst with joy. The feeling of those little bodies hugging him tightly, both trying to tell him about everything, was incomparable to anything else on the planet—even if his wife's eyes shot cold daggers at him.

Having never been home from downrange for longer than a few weeks, he knew the permanent adjustment would take a bit longer and hoped he was up for the challenge. He showered and, ignoring the hamper, zipped his laundry and toiletries back into his duffel bag, unsure of exactly where he belonged in his family's new house—if anywhere.

Opening the door, he nearly tripped over Owen sitting in the hall. Thankful for quick and calm reflexes, Ford smiled at the boy. "You could have come on in if you needed to, son."

Owen shook his head. "There's another bathroom. I was just waiting for you."

Ford rested a hand on Owen's shoulder as the boy preceded him down the hall. "Would you put my bag somewhere your mother won't trip over it?" Owen laughed at that and disappeared, dragging the bag with both hands.

In the open front room that was both living room and kitchen, Ford paused, taking in the scene.

Katie stood at the open fridge, laughing at something Miri said while she took out sandwich fixings and scolded the puppy. Scarlett sat on the countertop, pulling a loaf of bread from a wooden box.

Watching his wife made him smile, so lighthearted with the kids, her shorts clinging to her body, her dark sable ponytail swaying about. It was a scene right out of his dreams.

Ford let out a breath he hadn't realized he was holding. He was here. He didn't have to wonder from afar if his family was okay, he didn't have to rage against the helplessness that had kept him from them in the last few months. He could see them for himself and found that he could truly breathe again.

"Hey, Daddy, we're making sammiches!" Miri skipped over to him and took his hand to tug him to the table.

"No Blue Moon beer here on the island, Dad, but Gabe will find you something new. He knows beer. Well, and other things," Owen said, coaxing the puppy from under the table and wrangling him into his crate.

Amused that the boy remembered his favored beer, Ford poured a glass of water from the pitcher on the table, draining it before refilling it and draining half of that, too.

He caught Katie's worried frown and gave her a small smile of what he hoped was reassurance.

Her expression softened slightly, but she looked away.

Ford literally ached to touch her. He longed to press his lips to the slight frown on her forehead, smooth away the worry. Not to mention she was sexy as hell in that ponytail and shorts—especially to a husband who'd been gone for so long. Every fiber of his being wanted her close to him, his hands and his heart echoing with emptiness.

Suppressing a sigh, he rubbed his own forehead and tried to keep up with the kids. It was time to try and adjust to the outside world.

*   *   *

Aware of his every move, practically his every breath, Katie wanted to stomp her foot childishly. She was angry, dammit, and feelings of tenderness or arousal were absolutely *not* welcome. But they were there. Oh, were they there.

Luckily, the kids kept up a steady chatter, and she was free to avoid him for the moment, busying her hands slicing bread from the freshly baked loaf and putting together sandwiches.

"Sunset!" Miriam cried suddenly, jumping up and heading for the door.

"Sunset," Scarlett echoed, scooting off her chair to follow her sister, half a 'sammich' fisted tightly in one hand.

Owen freed Scout, and all three kids ran out the always-open front door.

"The sunset over the water is an event here," Katie explained, sticking the sandwiches into a bag and grabbing a leash from the hook by the door.

"Okay." Ford drained his water glass again and turned to follow his family.

Katie handed him two water bottles, which he tucked into the pockets of his cargo shorts with a wink.

She glanced away from him quickly, hopefully before he could see the smile she'd just suppressed.

The kids running ahead, the two walked in silence across the road in front of the house, through an open air market in the park and down a sandy path to the beach. The bar down the beach glowed brightly in the gathering dusk, faint music carrying on the breeze.

His steps slowing, Ford lightly caught Katie's fingers in his. The electric shock at his touch went straight through her body from head to toe, leaving a trail of fire that pooled low in her belly. Katie stopped short, chewing her lip, refusing to meet his eyes. Those eyes were always her undoing, as she could read his every emotion in them.

"I'm so sorry," he whispered, his thumb stroking her wrist, the motion familiar and comforting.

Her bottom lip quivered before she caught it in her teeth. "It's not all on you."

"Why do I not feel like you believe that?"

Katie simply stared at him then looked away, jerking her fingers from his to continue walking. His genuine confusion made her acutely aware of her own confusion. Nothing made sense right now.

* * *

Ford shoved his hands in his pockets and turned around, desperately wanting to walk the other way and be alone for awhile. To do that, though, would disappoint the kids who were jumping about on the shore, calling for him. Turning back to follow his wife just as the sun began to set, he stopped mid-stride.

The stunning oranges, pinks and purples exploded across the horizon, bathing the whole world in an amber glow that faded to a deep indigo as the sun sank into the sea. It was a sight to behold, to say the least. Even the kids stopped calling out, instead chorusing, "Oooo, aaahhh, oooo, aaahhh."

Ford waved in response to Miri's call, "See it, Daddy? See it?"

Walking closer, he felt a tug on his hand and looked down to see the tawny top of Scarlett's head. She didn't look at him, but her small hand slipped around two of his fingers. He stopped and sat cross-legged in the sand, letting the view in front of him soothe as only an ocean sunset can. Well, an ocean sunset and a small daughter, to be exact. Scarlett crawled into his lap, leaning back against him trustingly.

Ford smiled slightly, brushing light brown strands from the side of her little face. They watched the last of the sun's rays disappear, the now darkening silver sea dotted with a few lights from boats and buoys, the little girl drifting off to sleep curled into her daddy's arms.

While things were far from good—and pretty much far from even being okay—this one moment was just a little bit of perfect that he'd hold close as long as he could.

CHAPTER TWO

A LOW GROAN slipped out as Ford lowered himself to the porch bench. Elbows on his knees, he dropped his head into his hands, rather astonished to find it still attached. It'd been throbbing mercilessly since he'd boarded the first plane—had that been only yesterday? Bedtime had taken what seemed like endless hours before the kids had finally gone to sleep, each one needing repeated reassurance that he'd still be there come morning. Oh, he would be here, but at the moment Ford wasn't sure there'd be much of him functional ever again.

"They can't believe you're actually here," Katie said from the shadows where she sat in the porch hammock.

"I can't believe it, either," he replied, his exhaustion weighing down every word. Exhausted from war, from worry, from pain, from loneliness, he had nothing left and only wanted to crawl into bed with his wife, to hold her and be held by her. Deciding he had nothing to lose, he spoke quietly. "Is it possible for us to just go to bed and think about all this tomorrow?"

"Sure. You can sleep in Owen's room. He prefers his hammock over the full size bed." She stood. "I'll show you."

Reaching out, Ford caught her by the waist before she could walk past him. She tensed and pulled back, but he held on.

* * *

Katie put her hands on Ford's shoulders, fully intending to push him back and keep walking. His hands at her hips held on a little tighter, his head falling forward against her belly with a deep, bone-weary sigh. A sigh she echoed. God, how she loved him.

Familiarity and longing—such sharp longing—had her fingers caressing his neck and slipping up into his hair. It had been years since his hair had been long enough to really run her fingers through, and doing so now evoked feelings of tenderness for the twenty-two year old he'd been then. The tightness she'd seen at the edge of his eyes and mouth today made her heart hurt for him. But she was so damn angry, her own hurt reaching down so deep that she wasn't sure their love was strong enough to fight through to the surface.

"You need to sleep. You can stay here tonight. Tomorrow I'll call the B&B down the road for a room."

Ford's head jerked up, his eyes blazing blue steel in the dim light. "Katie, there's a hell of a lot to talk about and three kids to think about. I want to be here."

Angrily, Katie pushed past him to sit on the porch step, trying to keep her voice low. "What if that's not what *I* want, Ford? What if I can't take you being here?"

She toyed with the shooting star pendant around her neck, rocking slightly, her breath harsh in the night's quiet.

When Ford moved to sit down beside her on the step, laying a hand over her tightly clasped fingers, she nearly threw herself into his arms.

As if he felt her thoughts, he slid his arm around her, pulling her close despite her unyielding stiffness. When he held her, when she breathed him in, all the shattered pieces tumbled into place. All the missing him over the years of deployments—the gripping fear she'd had for him every hour of every day he was gone, the nearly single parenting through so much—it was all so close to crashing down around her now that he was here. His arms were steady and strong as always, his chest broad and warm. He smelled so good, his familiar woodsy scent enveloping her.

With a sigh, Katie forced herself to pull free and stood up. She loved him, but she couldn't need him like that again. She couldn't risk it.

"You need sleep."

With a sigh to match hers, he rose and followed her inside the house.

In their son's bedroom, Ford sat on the edge of the bed watching her cover their gangly nine-year-old, the hammock he sprawled in swinging slightly.

"Katie."

She couldn't stand it anymore.

He was here, he was finally here. The next thing she knew, Katie was kneeling in front of him, her arms wrapped tightly around him, holding him close and trying for closer.

"Jesus, Katie." His breath whooshed out at her sudden, fierce hug, his arms going around her just as tightly.

Her hands traveled over and over his back, assuring herself that he was really okay, really here.

"My God. You're here. You're safe." She whispered it against his chest several times, as if chanting the words would make it really true, once and for all.

As fast as it happened, it was over. Katie got to her feet and turned to leave the room.

Pausing in the doorway she took a deep breath and let it out slowly. "One step at a time?"

Ford nodded, looking so incredibly weary it was tough to turn away from him and close the door behind her.

But turn away she did.

*   *   *

Ford woke suddenly in the predawn darkness, his breathing harsh, sweat cooling on his body, but he found his bearings quickly. He'd had several months of life out of the field as he recuperated in the hospital, but as anyone who'd been in combat knew, it took far longer than that to adjust to said life. One thing he'd managed to do, so far, was to orient himself rather quickly upon awakening from the less intense of the nightmares. He lay still, letting the sounds around him calm him as his breathing returned to normal.

He could hear Owen's sleepy murmurs and sighs, the puppy's mid-dream yips from his crate, the ocean's steady beat—all comforting sounds.

Needing to move, Ford pulled a t-shirt on over his gym shorts and quietly left the room. The nearly ever-present dull headache had lessened after a few hours of sleep. Fresh air and a strong cup of coffee would help even further.

New to the house, he stood still and assessed the kitchen, breathing a sigh of relief that his wife's insistent need for coffee even before she woke fully hadn't changed. Indicator lights on a shiny red coffeepot showed it was set to brew automatically in a couple of hours. A few fumbling button pushes later, he was rewarded with the scent of fresh coffee as the pot began to fill. The dim light over the stove let him see two mugs waiting next to the brewing coffee. The fact that Katie had set out a mug for him next to hers warmed him inside, not to mention it allowed him to get the coffee with minimal noise.

With the mug full of coffee, black and strong, he moved silently to the screen door, disturbed that it was secured only with a high hook-and-eye latch. Ford eased his way out and sat on the porch step, cradling the coffee in both hands. Filling his lungs with the sea air, he felt the ever-present tightly coiled tension deep inside him begin to ease just a bit more. While he'd expected things to be very different, having come home to a foreign place and an all new reality, he'd certainly come home to more dramatic changes than he'd ever imagined. It all put him at a loss as to what to do.

* * *

With maternal ears tuned to the noises of the house, Katie heard Ford moving about the kitchen and the sound of the screen door opening before everything was again quiet. She'd pushed back the sheet and put her feet to the floor before realizing that going to him wasn't behavior of a wife who wanted a separation. It had sure been easier to hold tight to her anger while he was half a planet away, to decide their marriage was over when she couldn't touch him or be touched by him. It'd been easier to say the hurt was insurmountable when he wasn't there, when she couldn't see her pain reflected in his eyes. He was here now, and the hurt flared afresh, yet she had an deep urge to go to him, to hold him, to hear all that had happened to him, to tell him everything he'd missed. To open the small mahogany box that was tucked away and share the contents with him. That urge was almost stronger than her pain. Almost. She touched her pendant fleetingly and pulled her feet back up into the bed.

A few moments after she heard him go out the front door, Katie gave up trying to go back to sleep and quietly slipped out the patio door from her room to sit out back.

The trees rustled, filled with sounds of the bats and birds, the tropical breeze soothing in the darkness. Leaning back, Katie looked up at the stars, finding the constellations Aquila the Eagle and Orion the Hunter easily—though not as clearly seen as they were in the States. These constellations were Ford's favorites, the stars an anchor in his orphan world for as long as he could remember. He'd first shown them to her from the rooftop of her apartment building in the city, the faint stars barely visible amid the light pollution. Later, just before he deployed for the first time, he'd taken her on a ride outside the city, showing her how bright the stars were away from the lights. From then on, he'd often mention Aquila and Orion, asking her if she'd seen them or lying under them with her. When the kids had come along, they'd done the same with them.

Katie sighed deeply, a weariness deep in her bones despite the idyllic island she now lived on. Orion. She fingered the tiny shooting star pendant around her neck. So much had happened in the past year. Too much.

CHAPTER THREE

AS SOON AS the morning sun's rays began to streak the sky with reds and golds, Ford put on running shoes and slipped back out the front door. Adjusting his earbuds, he set off across the park to the beach. Once he had gotten back on his feet after the blast injuries, Ford had started running again as soon as he could. First the treadmill, then all over the hospital campus, followed by the base and the city itself. Coupled with pounding music, running was one of the things that empowered him and quieted the noise in his head. It even seemed to help the headache for a while, most days.

Ford ran along the shore for a few miles, appreciating the glorious many-hued sunrise over the shimmering blue water as a handful of colorful fishing boats headed out to sea. Boats. If they were going to live here, he'd have to learn about boats along with the kids. Island kids needed to know about boats, about the sea. He was a Midwesterner, what he knew about boats was confined to fishing in the rivers, not oceans. Maybe that Gabe guy Owen kept talking about could point him in the right direction.

His first sight of a helicopter on the horizon since he'd come to the island slowed his pace and brought him to a standstill. Tugging the earbuds free, he shaded his eyes with one hand and watched the helo approach. A bright splash of colors against the blue morning sky, the tourist helicopter looked nothing like the Blackhawk he'd had under his hands so many times, yet the whipping of the blades brought him a flashback of fresh stings from blowing sand and the blinding sunlight that seemed to pierce the skull even from behind shades.

Watching the helo disappear over the trees, Ford looked around. Aside from his racing heart and sweaty hands, everything went on as it should. Fishing boats moved on the water, a black dog ran ahead of a woman and two children walking up the beach. He calmed his breathing and stood up fully. His counselor at the hospital had warned him that flashbacks could happen differently out in the real world as opposed to the hospital's sequestered halls or the sheltered life he'd led while recovering on base. While it had unsettled him, this one had felt like an adrenaline surge with a memory flash. The doctor had also assured him that flashbacks while reacclimating to civilian life did not necessarily equal Post Traumatic Stress Disorder, that while he needed to be aware of PTSD signs, he'd checked out so far.

Turning around, Ford ran back down the beach, nodding at the girl now frolicking in ankle deep water with the dog while the woman swung the smaller child about, both of them laughing.

He ran past The Painted Parrot, the shades lowered, the seats empty. He ran until his muscles burned and his stomach protested the lack of breakfast fuel before he turned and headed back up the beach. The sea breeze was a balm breathed in deeply over and over. Ford savored the salty air. He'd probably never get used to it after the sand-filled air he'd breathed for so long downrange. He slowed to a walk, cooling down his overheated muscles as he approached the robin's egg blue house.

His wife—she *was* still his wife—sat on the front step, a coffee mug in her hands and another mug plus a water bottle at her side. Despite her aloof expression and the huge wall between them, the sight of her waiting for him fanned the flickers of hope stirring inside him. Maybe her love for him wasn't as easily dismissed as she seemed to want.

* * *

Watching him run across the park and approach the house, Katie couldn't suppress the surge of love that washed over her. For nearly ten years, this man had been what defined home for her, and the feeling of safety from being by his side or in his arms had made the fear from her terrible early years fade. Together they'd made a safe place for the both of them, a place strong enough to set aside their devastating childhoods, strong enough to weather deployment during war, time and again. Or so she'd thought.

Shaking off the dark cloud as Ford drew closer, Katie thought he looked less fiercely intent this morning.

His eyes were clear and open instead of narrowed against pain or noise, one winking at her as he accepted the water bottle she held out. He dropped to the step beside her, draining the bottle before picking up the steaming coffee. He sipped with a sound of appreciation that coffee addicts everywhere would understand.

"Scarlett is rather put out with you already this morning." Her slight smile took the sting from the words.

"I thought I'd be back before she noticed." Ford grimaced, turning his head to look through the doorway. "I'm a little out of touch, huh?"

"You know it's like riding a bike. She's momentarily mollified with cookies for breakfast in our—my—bed."

He didn't speak, sipped the coffee, his eyes closing briefly in further appreciation.

"How long did it take before you could run again?" The question surprised her as much as it seemed to catch him off guard. She hadn't planned to bring up anything about their most recent time apart anytime soon, but it was hard to maintain distance—emotional and physical—from him, despite her simmering anger.

"Once I was on my feet, about three months."

"Until you were on your feet?" Her voice shook slightly, her gaze on the brightly colored banners in the park's open air market.

He took a deep breath, letting it hiss out slowly between his teeth. "Three months—one month totally flat, two more months from a chair."

Katie's hand flew to her mouth. What a living hell for any man, especially one who hated laying flat—he'd always used two fat pillows, minimum—and was never still for long at any given moment. While she'd gotten formal medical reports via email, the day to day things he went through had fallen victim to the near silence between them for all those months.

Ford's mouth twisted wryly. "You'd think being helpless would make a guy more grateful than I have been."

"I can't imagine what I'd think, Ford." Katie shook her head and looked down at the ground, her shoulder length hair falling in a curtain to hide her face.

He reached over and tucked the silky strands behind her ear, his big hand lingering at her jaw, the gentle touch urging her to look at him. The shadows in his eyes made them dark and brought tears to hers.

"I needed you too much, Katiebean. So much that I feared I'd break you with it. I couldn't..." He trailed off, dropping his hand and his gaze.

"If only—"

"DaddyDaddyDaddy! There you are!" Scarlett fairly flew out the door and into his lap. Her shyness hadn't lasted long, this precocious girl.

"Whoa, Biscuit." He quickly caught her before she tumbled off. Chocolate brown eyes just like Katie's looked at him accusingly. She squinted then, her small hand coming up to rub the scar on his forehead. "Did a bad man hurt you like Harry?"

Ford stifled a laugh and took the little hand in his, kissing it before he stood with her in his arms. "Something like that, but it's all good now. And, come to think of it, I do have magic."

"You do?" Her eyes widened.

Katie laughed at Scarlett's expression, shaking off the heavy moment the child had interrupted. "Magic, you say?"

Ford nodded, "I have a magic pocket in my duffel bag where surprises for little girls and boys show up."

Scarlett's legs kicked to get down and, once her feet were on the porch, she darted inside, yelling at the top of her lungs, "Daddy has a magic pocket, Miri! Owen! OoooWEN!"

Ford rubbed his inner thigh ruefully. "She grew, I gotta remember where her feet hit."

"Magic pocket?" Katie snickered, clapping a hand over her mouth as giggles bubbled up.

Ford leaned in close, his lips just a breath away from hers. "Oh, yeah." He drew out the words in a growl, nuzzling her neck playfully.

Caught in the moment, Katie giggled helplessly, grasping his shoulders for balance. She closed her eyes as hot need rushed through her. She badly wanted to lean into him, to stoke the fires flared—but the gulf between them was just too big. She dropped her hands and backed up a step.

Ford sighed and turned to follow Scarlett inside. Turning a three—almost-four—year old loose with his bag would mean an empty bag in two seconds flat. It was probably too late.

Katie watched him go, her bottom lip caught in her teeth, her arms wrapped around her body. The damp t-shirt he'd worn running hung over one shoulder, his broad, muscular back sporting scars—some old, some fresh. A startling new one ran from just below his shoulder blade to the top of his hip, still pink and slightly raised. She wanted to ask him about that scar, about his injuries, about everything that had happened to him in the past year. Her anger wouldn't let her hear him out, didn't want her to understand. While she yearned to share the burden of all that had happened in Ford's absence, she knew that once they started talking about it, the secret tucked away deep in her heart and soul would no longer be safe. Katie wasn't sure she'd—they'd—survive bringing it out.

CHAPTER FOUR

"SUNSET!" Katie called from the kitchen, smiling at the predicted effect of her words as the kids whooped and ran in from the backyard en masse. She handed Miri a bakery box and Scarlett a lightweight bag while Owen pocketed the puppy's rarely-used leash, along with a handful of puppy treats, and led the charge out the front door.

Pausing to brush and re-ponytail her hair, Katie realized she hadn't seen Ford since he'd said he was going for a run more than three hours ago. She couldn't help but worry about him. Military spouses heard plenty about what to be aware of when their soldier returned home—and plenty of hard stories, too. Despite—or maybe more so because of—the issues between them, Katie was concerned about Ford. He was quiet much of the time, his eyes narrowed slightly against what she knew was both pain and the noise around him. He ran twice and sometimes three times a day, drank water like it was his last chance and hardly slept that she could tell. She hoped he'd show up at the sunset, for she wanted to lay eyes on him as well as introduce him to her friends. Even if she wasn't particularly hospitable to him right now, they would rally around him like they had around her and the kids since their arrival on the island.

* * *

Just as the sun performed its finale, sinking into the sea with a burst of lavender and orange, the sky flushing indigo, Ford ended his run in a walk amid shrieks and calls from his offspring and apparently the rest of the island's offspring as well.

Oblivious to the sweat that plastered his shirt to his body, Scarlett climbed him and kissed his cheek soundly.

Miri, hand in hand with a gray-eyed girl whose name she said was Rory, told him about the cookies she'd helped Katie decorate and how two, maybe three of them had his name on them.

"I drew it on there myself," she said proudly, smiling from ear to ear when Ford expressed his astonishment that he had his very own cookies waiting.

Owen called out from the water's edge where he and several other children chased the puppy and the black dog Ford had seen the other morning.

Amid all of that, Ford winced suddenly as the hairs on his leg were mercilessly tugged. Resisting the urge to shake his leg, he looked down to find a tow-headed baby's fists clutching said leg hairs as he pulled himself to a wobbly stand. With a grin, Ford scooped up the sandy baby with his free arm. "Look what I found, a tiny sea urchin," he told Scarlett, who giggled and rubbed the baby's head.

"That's not a nurchin, that's Baby Zane."

"Hey, you must be Ford." A man came up and took the baby and swung the tot high in the air, bringing forth shrieks from both the baby and Scarlett.

"Nash, father of the urchin." He tucked the baby against his side and clasped Ford's outreached hand in a firm shake. "Nice to have a face with the legend." He grinned, his friendly demeanor welcoming.

Ford snorted. "Legend, he says."

"Owen has regaled us with stories about his dad every single day since he got here. His sisters have too, but that boy? He's your champion, my man." Nash clapped a hand to Ford's shoulder as they approached the picnic table surrounded by brightly colored umbrellas and beach chairs.

Ford's reflexive shift at the contact to his once tender shoulder went unnoticed as Nash plopped the baby into a playpen where his wail of protest turned to giggles when Scarlett climbed over the side to join him. Nash's attention was diverted by a couple walking by commenting on his Painted Parrot Charters t-shirt and asking about a morning boat ride.

Ford stood at the edge of the scattered gathering, watching Katie laugh and reach out both hands to rumple through another woman's short blond hair that was apparently the subject of their conversation. His wife took his breath away any time, but never more so than when she laughed. The first time he'd heard that laugh, he'd made it his mission in life to make it happen every day.

Her eyes meeting his, Katie motioned him over.

When he came to stand beside her, Katie said, "This is Jill. She belongs to those two you just met over there. She's been invaluable to me since we moved here."

He saw the other woman smile and speak to him, but his entire being was focused on the warmth of Katie's hand resting naturally at his lower back. He let himself lean just a little closer so their bodies brushed together, the contact sending a welcome, familiar sizzle all up and down his side. Pulling his focus forward, Ford apparently managed to make the right noises as the other woman patted his arm and moved away to check on the baby.

"Have you been running the whole time since you left the house?" Katie turned to face him, her eyes traveling over his damp hair and sweat-soaked shirt.

Ford ran a hand over his hair and wiped it on his shorts. "Along with a little recon—exploring." Civilian language, Ford, civilian language, he reminded himself.

Before Katie could reply, Miri appeared at her elbow. "Daddy, here's your cookie." The girl handed Ford a sugar cookie, a wobbly 'Daddy' spelled out in bright blue icing across it.

Ford grinned, tapping his daughter's nose and breaking the cookie in two. "Share it with me, Miribelle."

Miri grinned, her lips instantly blue as she bit into the cookie.

Next to her, Rory grinned, her lips blue, too. "Blue is the best icing." The two scampered off before Ford could agree.

He saw that Katie had been commandeered to fill paper cups with something red and no doubt sickly sweet, leaving him to his own devices for the moment.

Polishing off his half of the cookie, he stifled the impulse to whirl around as he felt the cold chill of a water bottle pressed against his arm.

"You looked hot." A man with dark gold hair, skin permanently sun-reddened stood next to him, handing over the bottle and shaking his hand. "Gabe Montgomery, I run The Painted Parrot."

Ford nodded, draining the bottle in two long gulps. "I owe you my thanks, I hear."

Eyebrow raised in question, Gabe wrapped an arm around a woman with riotous curls pulled back from her face as she came to his side.

"I've heard how much you and Charlie have helped my family," Ford said.

The woman at Gabe's side smiled, her eyes assessing him. "We love Katie and the kids, so glad they're happy here."

Ford wondered if the edge of warning in her voice was his imagination or if Charlie was putting him on notice.

"It's us who owe you thanks for your service, Ford," Gabe replied, Charlie nodding in agreement. With a squeeze to Ford's arm and a kiss to Gabe's cheek, she moved away to scoop up a runaway Baby Zane and swoop in to dip his toes in the water, eliciting squeals and giggles, drawing several of the other kids to join her. It seemed that child was the island's favorite mascot.

Ford joined Gabe and Nash along with several others in a pickup game of volleyball followed by chasing the kids in and out of the water, carrying an armful of kids out a few feet into the sea and dropping them, much to their delight.

The evening light waned, the stars blinking to life in the darkening sky, the outlines of boats on the water growing fainter. Down the beach a little way, The Painted Parrot's lights danced as music drifted on the breeze. Torches were lit and a bonfire started as more food appeared from various baskets and containers.

Kicked back in a low-slung beach chair with his arm hanging over the side, Ford sifted sand between his fingers, marveling at how different yet the same sand felt from one side of the world to the other. The sand in Afghanistan was rough and grating while this sand was smooth, whispering between his fingers. Was that a real tactile difference, or was it the mindset? Seems like the ocean would smooth the sand here, he mused, closing his fist around a handful.

"And this is just any old evening here in Paradise," Nash commented, dropping into a beach chair next to Ford.

Nash eyed the other man's hand in the sand. "Sandman dreams?"

Ford snorted. "You might say that."

"Jill says take this troublemaker." Rory ran up to Nash, a protesting Zane in her arms. She was gone almost before the boy hit Nash's lap.

With a grunt, Nash caught the baby and spun him around.

Zane's protesting wail was cut off by a giggle as Nash swung him high, bringing him down to blow kisses on the marshmallow sticky cheeks. "Troublemaker? Why you even taste like sugar." The baby's giggles erupted into full blown belly laughs, making both men laugh, too.

"Bet you're more than ready to go up in a helo again," Nash commented. The other man hadn't moved, except for his hand in the sand.

Ford lifted his other hand and let it fall with a shrug. "Yes and no."

"I think I get that. Part of me will always—and I mean always—be tugging at the bit to rush into a fire."

They sat in comfortable silence, the baby snuggling into the crook of Nash's arm, his little eyes heavy.

They watched their family and friends, the island's peace blanketed in twilight's glow.

Gabe stood in silhouette against the sky, roasting a marshmallow with an arm around Charlie. She laughed at something he'd dipped his head to whisper in her ear.

Katie and Reggie, the kids and few other adults had run down to the volleyball net, leaving the fire in Gabe's hands. Scattered around the fire, people sat in chairs and on blankets, a hush falling over them in the growing darkness, the shouts and laughs from the volleyball players combined with the faint music spilling from The Painted Parrot.

Ford sighed, eternally working on becoming accustomed to that odd combination of being simultaneously relaxed and alert. As a soldier in the field, alert and on edge is a way of life. As a soldier at home—a husband, a father, a friend—on edge needed to be downgraded significantly to merely alert for the people he cared about.

"There you are, Daddy." Scarlett, heavy-eyed, with chocolate streaking her face, appeared at Ford's knee.

"Here I am, Biscuit." Ford smiled, his heart squeezing as it did every time he looked at this child. She'd gone from toddler to little person in the year he'd been gone, reminding him of just how much he'd missed. Lifting the little girl onto his lap, she was nearly asleep before he'd settled back into the chair.

The two men and two babies lapsed into comfortable silence, the warm weight of cuddly babies coupled with the ocean's rhythm hypnotic as the night deepened next to the sea.

Paradise, indeed.

CHAPTER FIVE

ROLLING THE WEIGHT of sleeping Scarlett from his arms into the bed next to her sister, Ford closed his eyes against the brief wave of dizziness that washed over him. He'd been on his feet for the better part of the past three days and was fading fast. Groaning slightly, he pushed himself up as Katie came into the room.

With a slight smile for him, she wiped both sleeping little girls' faces with a soft cloth, washing away the chocolate smears and marshmallow stickiness.

Ford left the room quietly, heading for the shower and bed in hopes of sleeping for at least a little while.

"Hey, Dad?" Owen's voice penetrated the fog taking over Ford's brain and body.

"Yeah, sport?"

"Nice night for stars." The boy's expression was so hopeful, Ford hadn't the heart to beg off.

Slinging an arm around his son's shoulders, Ford turned in the direction of the back door. "Lead the way." Owen's grin was priceless, worth the effort of Ford's drawing up of the last dredges of his strength.

* * *

From the doorway of the girls' room, Katie watched them go, their firstborn's face alight as he talked about the stars with his father.

Gazing at Ford's beloved night skies had become a thing between him and Owen almost instantly, Katie remembered, with Ford swaddling a tiny boy while lying out on a blanket on the apartment building roof in the city where maybe ten stars could be seen if you were lucky.

"The best view is down on the beach away from all the lights, of course, but it's not a bad view from here," Owen said, flopping down on an old quilt already on the ground.

Squashing up the pillow into a ball, Ford stretched out next to the boy, swallowing a groan at finally lying down.

They lay in silence for a few moments, the stars slowly showing themselves as their eyes adjusted. A leg draped over his father's, Owen leaned his head close and pointed. "Aquila the Eagle." His finger followed the constellation. His other hand came up. "Orion the Hunter. I was surprised we could see both of them after Mom moved us here."

"Same here when I got to the Sandbox in the Middle East. I was so excited to know I could still see them. I used to look up out there and think about you and your Mom and your sisters seeing the same stars. It helped me not seem so far away." Ford's voice was husky with fatigue.

Owen scooted closer, his head on Ford's shoulder as they stargazed, murmuring tidbits from time to time, exclaiming at a shooting star that left a blaze of orange and blue across the sky.

"When do you go back, Dad?" Owen asked sleepily.

Ford's arm came around the boy, pulling him in close. "I don't. I'm home."

Owen didn't reply, having drifted off to sleep, his body heavy against Ford's.

Ford tried to relax into the island night. His overly fatigued body pulled at him, his eyes closing almost against his will. With his daughters and his wife safely sleeping in the cottage, his son nestled against his side, The Crackerjack Flying Ace let the blessed oblivion of sleep overtake him.

CHAPTER SIX

OPENING THE DOOR to the bakery, Ford's steps faltered. Katie stood between the arms of a dark-haired man as she held up a brightly colored cupcake wall decoration for him to hang in place. They were both laughing, Katie lightly punching the man's side as she let him take over the job.

"Why didn't you do what I told you to do in the first place, Luke? I know what I'm talking about."

The man laughed again as Katie stepped out from under his arms while he hung the cupcake up where she'd indicated. Ford frowned at the camaraderie between his wife and this man, letting the bakery door swing closed behind him, the bell ringing out.

Turning, Katie met him with a questioning look. Telling him all he had to do was let her know if he left the house as the kids were used to finding her at the bakery next door, she'd come to work early, anxious to get the bakery remodel finished and get back to business. With the money she'd saved in the first few months plus Amos's insistent help—as the bakery had first been his wife's for many years—she'd managed to make the shop a perfect combination of her heritage as well as her own style. She couldn't wait to re-open the doors, even though it had barely been a week since she'd closed them for the fast remodel.

Before she could ask, Ford said, "Charlie stopped by and took them all with her to help somebody do something? At least I think that's what went down, it got kinda crazy when she came in and the next thing I knew she was walking away waving, all the kids running off in front of her. I came by to be sure that was okay." Ford rubbed his forehead absently.

Katie nodded. "It's always okay when it comes to Charlie. Or Jill. Or Reggie."

She admired the wall, addressing the other man as he picked up his toolbox. "I appreciate your help as always, Luke."

Luke returned her hug, one-armed, and turned to Ford, holding out his hand. "Welcome home. Luke Branson."

Ford shook the other man's hand. "Ford Callahan."

"When he's not moonlighting as a handyman, Luke is the local sheriff," Katie told Ford, avoiding his eyes as she brushed the countertop with one hand.

"C'mon down to The Painted Parrot soon, throw some darts, meet some folks," Luke invited, his expression friendly and open.

"I just might do that," Ford said, his tone more terse than he'd intended.

The other man didn't seem to notice, hefting the toolbox to one hand, whistling as he left the bakery.

"I can do things for you around here, you know. No need for him to be hanging about." The words were out of his mouth before Ford could stop them.

Katie looked at him like he'd grown two heads or something. She didn't say a word, making him resist the urge to squirm under her laser stare. How could women do that, simply stare at a guy and make him want to confess to things he didn't even know he'd done?

"Luke is a friend, one of several that have helped the kids and I get settled." Her voice was oddly flat, not angry or even really irritated. That bothered Ford much more than a shouting match would have. Cold and detached is never a good thing in a marriage.

He changed tactics, hoping she'd ignore his jealous outburst. "Tell me what I can do to help, I need to do something."

Katie waved him away. "Take time for yourself, go walk the beach, get a drink. You're on leave, not to mention you know how rare kid-free moments are."

He inclined his head. "I do. Come walk with me?" Expecting that she'd wave him off again, make some excuse or send him on an errand away from her, Ford was taken aback when she nodded.

"I could use a beach walk." Katie pocketed her phone and locked the bakery door.

* * *

Katie had to concede—if only to herself—that forcing him away from her as much as possible wasn't practical nor was it fair to either of them. Driving him away really didn't solve anything, so she'd be civil. She figured they could use this walk to set some ground rules. That way, when things didn't work out, Ford would have to face the truth rather than blame her hostility. The truth that they were over.

The sea breeze tousled her ponytail as they walked across the park, down to the sand. Pausing to kick off her shoes, Katie looked up to see Ford standing still, watching the helicopter fly across the sky in front of them.

She said, "Tourists mostly—there's an air ambulance when someone needs one."

Ford nodded, shading his eyes against the sun as he watched the helicopter circle back, people eagerly peering out, the pilot pointing.

"You miss it."

"I can feel the stick in my hands." He held up loose fists, pantomiming flying. "Makes my feet twitch, too." His smile was genuine, if a little strained.

"Itching to get back aboard?" Katie asked. She knew every deployment brought treasured home time for Ford but also a persistent nudge to return to the skies that began anew the moment his feet touched the ground. He loved his job and did it well, saving lives and helping others who saved lives with a single-minded passion and skill reserved for few top notch pilots. She'd heard the stories—he was one of the best.

Ford shook his head as they walked along the shore, his gaze on the dolphins dancing on the waves, the spray they kicked up in the air glittering like jewels in the sunlight. He cleared his throat. "No. No itch, just deeply ingrained habit. I meant it when I said I'm out."

"The Army is all you've known—all we've known," Katie replied, walking in the edge of the water, the waves rolling over her feet. Before coming to the island last year, she'd never known how the sea grounded her. She now knew it was because of her heritage, of her grandparents Amos and Bessie, and the estranged, yet deep,

connection her family had with this island. When she'd moved here
with the kids, the first time the sea had swirled over her feet, pulling
her against the sand, she'd known this was it. This was her personal
ley line.

"There's more to us than military life." Ford bent to pick up a
shell in shades of ivory and peach, beautiful but with a jagged,
broken edge. "Like this. An amazing creation, no less beautiful for its
jagged edges."

Katie looked at the shell, then up into his face. The Katie he
knew grinned, "That was almost poetry, Ace."

Ford chuckled, pocketing the shell carefully.

They walked in silence away from The Painted Parrot and the
busier part of the beach where a volleyball game was setting up and
families dabbled at the edge of the water, filling brightly colored
buckets alongside children that darted in and out of the water's edge.

Before Katie could gather up her courage to draw some lines in
the sand, so to speak, Ford stopped and turned to face her.

He shoved his hands in his cargo pockets as if to keep from
grasping her hands in his. "I know you're convinced that we've done
too much damage to each other. But, Katie, we're stronger than this.
As kids, we both fought through so much before we even met. Then
those two desperate kids with a baby on the way, a deployment
looming and fifteen dollars in their pockets took on the world. We
built the family we'd never had." With that, he took a dull gold token
from his pocket and handed it to her, folding her hand over it with a
squeeze. "We have a history, Katiebean, don't throw it away."

She took the token, letting her fingers linger under his for a
moment then pocketing the trinket from the boardwalk arcade he
used take her to once in a while, back in the days when pennies were
precious and few. She turned to look out to sea, her gaze following a
multicolored sailboat, dolphins in its wake.

"Ford, those kids had each other. It was them against the world. I
can't pretend that's still us."

"I don't believe it's pretend, Katie." He touched her arm, urging
her to face him. "Can't one decision made in pain and stupidity
cancel out the other decision made in pain and stupidity? Aren't we
worth a fresh start?"

"You're healed, you're home, that would seem like a fresh start." Katie brought her hands up to redo her ponytail as she again faced the water. "But," she took a deep, shaky breath, "I just don't know."

He grabbed her hands in both of his, shaking them, bending his head to look into her eyes. His blue ones were stormy, but with more fear than anger. "Katie, I didn't know what else to do. I couldn't move without screaming or passing out unless I was drugged. I couldn't hold a single thought in my head. I'm not making excuses, I'm telling you how it was. Even so, sometimes I think it was the pain of not being with you that kept me down, it was that pain I had to work through to get upright again. Logically I know better, but I wonder."

"But you wouldn't let me help you," she grated out, low and tight, pulling her hands from his.

"You didn't need a husband who could only writhe in his own agony. I couldn't put that burden on you."

Katie paced back and forth on the sand, wrapping her arms around her body, trying to keep from flying apart. Again.

With both hearts breaking for the pain they'd caused each other, they faced the sea, lost in their own thoughts.

"I'm so sorry, but I did what I thought best." His voice was hoarse, barely audible over the sound of the waves.

"What *you* thought best. You didn't even consult me, Ford. As soon as you were stateside, I flew to the hospital. I packed up the kids and showed up for you without hesitation. I fully intended to stay in the Fisher House nearby for as long as it took to get you home—or closer to home. I had even arranged for childcare help while we were there. That's what a marriage is, Ford. And you know what? Despite your helplessness of the moment, I needed you. *You*, Ford—however I could get you. You have no idea how I needed you."

"Fuck." Ford stalked away a few steps and turned back. His frustration spilled over. "I'm right here!" he shouted, waving his arms in the air. "Right here. As soon as I could be the man you need, I came home."

Unflinching in the face of his shouts, Katie snarled at him, "No. No, Ford. The man I need is the one I tried to reach the day the world flew apart. The man I need is the one the Army told me might not live through the night, night after night. The one who convinced me to marry him and give our baby a shot at a real family. Who laughed with joy and strutted with pride when we got pregnant again and then again." She stomped to him, giving him a shove that only bounced off his solid chest. "The dying man whose side I couldn't get to because—I couldn't get to when he was blown to bits. That's the man I married. That man is dead to me. This one?" She gestured to him, a hand waving up and down. "This one chose to turn his back on me."

With that, she walked the other way, tossing her hair into the wind behind her. If she could just push him away with her righteous anger, her secret would remain buried and he'd never have to experience the agonizing pain she carried. She could protect him from that—by losing him for good.

CHAPTER SEVEN

FORD STOOD WATCHING Katie's retreat, her ponytail whipping around in the breeze. He was *dead* to her? What the hell was he supposed to do with that? Because grabbing her and kissing her senseless, showing her just how fucking dead he was *not*, probably wouldn't go over well. He growled his frustration, running his hands through his hair and back again. He didn't drink much these days—after the bouts with pain pills followed by the discovery that the all-too-easy oblivion of getting blind drunk brought relief from the noise in his head—but damn it all, if this wasn't a drinking time he didn't know what was.

Rubbing his forehead gingerly, Ford strode across the sand to The Painted Parrot, muttering the whole way. Dead to her—really? Did she realize how close he'd come to actually *being dead*? He shook his head, growling again. Oblivious to the intimidating figure he made in the crowded lunchtime bar, Ford stalked across the room and slid onto the farthest barstool, turning so his back was against the wall. Dropping his head back, he closed his eyes for a moment, hoping the faint buzzing sound that often warned of a full blown duck-and-cover migraine event would be wrong for a change.

Behind the bar, Gabe had seen Ford's fierce approach across the room. Exchanging glances with his business partner and best friend who'd stopped by to talk over the charter schedule, Gabe served a couple of customers and made his way to the bar's end. With practiced ease, Nash left his seat and took Gabe's place, bantering with customers without missing a beat. Being Katie's friends meant the two men had automatically been looking out for her husband, especially knowing what they both knew about soldiers returning from a war zone.

Gabe set a cold bottle of beer in front Ford with a thump, a glass of water alongside it.

Opening one eye, Ford raised a brow.

Gabe pushed the drinks closer. "Water is all I've seen you drink so far and Blue Moon is what Owen has asked me weekly if I have in stock for his dad."

The mention of his son cracked Ford's stony expression. He drained half the beer in a long gulp, then held the cool bottle against his forehead.

"Tough morning?" Gabe refilled his own glass with his favored house-made lemonade. While he wasn't a combat veteran himself, he'd known plenty of them during his firefighting days and knew reacclimation could be a massive challenge for any soldier. He'd been first-hand witness to more than one crash and burn upon reentry to civilian life.

Hissing out a sigh, Ford leaned both elbows on the bar, resting his mouth against his clasped hands.

"I—" He stopped, holding out his empty hands, elbows still on the bar.

Gabe wiped down the bar in front of a newly vacated seat. "Nash and I are taking the *JohnBToo* out here in a few, why don't you come with us?"

Ford shook his head, finishing off both the beer and the water. "Thanks, but I'm not good company."

"No need to be good company. We could use your observation skills. Yesterday the kids told me they saw smoke in the east. So we're going to take a look around some of the more out of the way spots." Gabe said, low voiced.

"Ya know, recon." Nash gave Ford a cheeky grin. "Step up, soldier."

Ford gave a small laugh, "Well, when you put it that way."

The three men were aboard the *JohnBToo* in minutes, the boat's cooler already stocked with drinks as well as snacks. As fishermen who ran charters, Gabe and Nash were prepared.

"Headache?" Nash asked, observing Ford rub his forehead for the third time in as many minutes.

"Always. Post concussive." Ford answered shortly, pulling his shades down from the top of his head.

"Oh, man, been there." Gabe groaned. "Took a roof beam to the head during a four-alarm fire midtown. Over a year before the echoes stopped and another year or so for the sudden flare ups." He shook his head, remembering all too well.

Gabe stood at the boat's wheel as they sped away from the shore out into the sea.

A trio of sighs went up as the sounds faded to only the boat, wind and sea.

They rode along in silence for a while before Nash pointed out Shelter Cove, a place locals loved and, by mutual agreement, kept largely hidden from the tourists. "The point of living out here is to be able to find complete solitude easily. This is one of many places where that can happen."

"I think the kids have mentioned Shelter Cove," Ford said, his eyes scanning the shoreline.

"Reggie brings them here often. Fun to explore and good fishing, too," Gabe remarked, bringing the boat around and back into the open water.

Ever the first responder and firefighter captain, Gabe saw when the tension in Ford's body began to loosen, the tightness around his mouth ease. Glancing at Nash, he saw his friend's slight nod. He'd noticed, too. Katie and the kids meant a lot to both men and they wanted to like her husband, wanted him to be okay. Turned out, Ford was a pretty easy guy to like.

Conversation was intermittent and idle, from fishing to island life, as they scouted the usual coves and points, still seeing nothing out of the ordinary.

"So, Ford, how's it been? Coming home?" Nash stepped up from the cabin below, tossing out packages of peanut butter and crackers to the other two men, cold drinks already in hand.

Ford snorted, neatly catching the package. "Aside from my wife saying I'm dead to her? Peachy."

"Ouch." Gabe grimaced.

"That's cold." Nash shivered. "What did you do?"

"Other than get blown to bits and refuse to come home?" Ford's mouth twisted wryly at hearing the words out loud.

"Cliff's Notes version, that," Gabe said.

Ford let out a long breath. "Long story short, I refused to come home to recover, and she considers that decision abandonment. She stopped talking to me eight months ago, only occasional email updates, the kids took my calls."

"What's your plan?" Gabe stood at the wheel, the sun glinting off his shades as he slowed the boat into another cove. Nash moved to stand against the opposite rail next to Ford, all three men scanning the shoreline as well as the waters of the cove.

"My only plan was to get home," Ford replied.

Satisfied that nothing seemed untoward, Gabe steered them back out into the open water.

"Well, that's mission accomplished, no?" Nash sat back on the bench seat, legs stretched out in front of him.

Ford clinked his bottle to the other man's. "I'm with my family, so yes."

"Are you working it out with her? Sleeping together?" Nash asked.

Behind his shades, Ford narrowed his eyes. "Without success. She tried to get me a room down the road the day I got here and has mentioned it a time or three since."

Gabe made a face at that. "That stings."

Ford nodded, pacing the boat's short deck. "You're telling me."

"Time for a new mission. I'd put my best moves on her all the time, brother. Brush up against her every chance you get, whisper in her ear. Remind her just how good it was—is." Nash grinned.

"I don't know. I think I'd give her some space, let her know you're sticking but don't suffocate her," Gabe countered.

"Lotta help the two of you are." Ford looked back and forth between the two men, yet thinking there was a ring of truth to both suggestions.

Before he could say as much, Gabe said it first, "Probably a mix between the two. Let her know you want her, but don't push too far."

"And there'll be a nice, big, red flashing light that'll mark 'too far,' right?" Ford scoffed.

"If only." Nash took over the boat's wheel at Gabe's signal.

Gabe picked up a pair of binoculars, scanning the shoreline. "Looks like a boat was pulled up over there recently."

Nash frowned. "This place is pretty isolated. Want to look closer?"

Gabe shook his head. "Let's remember it, come back and look around on foot."

"Most of these islands are uninhabited?" Ford took the binoculars from Gabe to look for himself.

"Right. Fiji is the biggest, then there's Vanua Levu, then us. After that, they're on the map but that's about all," Nash answered, steering them back out into the open sea, headed for home.

"If that's the case, how can you be on the lookout for trouble?" Ford frowned.

"Welcome to island living. Once off the populated islands, it's all fair game. But you know how every place has its rhythms once you get familiar." Gabe stood next to Nash, reaching out for the other man to let him have the wheel back.

"Bossy." Nash held his ground, forcing Gabe to shove him slightly before he relinquished control.

"He always like that?" Ford sat with his head tipped back, letting the sun and wind work their magic.

"Bossy as hell, always has been." Nash dropped beside Ford for the ride back.

Gabe adjusted his shades and settled his stance. "When ya got it, ya got it." His laugh blended with the groans of the other two men.

CHAPTER EIGHT

THE DAYS PASSED in sunshine and sand, with Ford joining Gabe and Nash on the boat a few mornings, sometimes running on the beach at sunrise, learning his way around the cheerful island by letting the kids tow him about, helping Luke and Katie finish up the last of the bakery remodel. His flashbacks were infrequent and handled surprisingly easily.

The kids learned that sometimes he tuned out, as Gabe called it when Ford had gone quiet the last time a helicopter flew over them—they'd all been on the beach with Gabe and Rory while Charlie and Katie ran a bridal shower in The Painted Parrot.

Ford was thankful his odd moments weren't full-on freak outs where he'd toss the kids to the ground and cover them with his body or something. He'd heard plenty of such stories and was admittedly fearful of scaring his kids—not that he hadn't had the instinctive urge to do something much like that, but so far he'd been clear-headed enough to know where he was and react accordingly.

While the kids seemed to be readily accepting of a second parental voice every time he returned home, Ford considered that the awkwardness between himself and Katie was partly a folly of military life, even without all the extra stuff they'd been through. He'd never been home long enough for his wife to adjust to having him in her daily life. In their entire marriage, his time at home had always been filled with vacations and holidays with a few low-key days thrown in before he'd returned to duty and Katie dealt with the every day without his presence. It dawned on him that he really had no idea how to live with them as a family, day in and day out. That fact complicated their already precarious situation.

After leaving him yet another sticky note with the B&B's address, Katie hadn't mentioned it again, but it was clear that she was carefully steering clear of being alone with him as much as possible. She spent the evenings after the kids were in bed over at the bakery. Sometimes she was alone, other times Ford saw Jill or Reggie join her from where he sat on the porch.

By that time of day, Ford's head usually insisted he go motionless for a while anyway, so he didn't invade her space. He was also hesitant to bring their problems into what he knew was a soothing place for her.

*　*　*

Katie reopened the bakery with a flourish, resuming the morning bread delivery with complimentary tarts made from kavika—sometimes called mountain apple—included in the delivery. Flaky and delicious, those barely palm-sized tarts made from the native, slightly sweet and sour fruit with a pale pink flesh were fast becoming a trademark.

Due to her late nights and early risings, the kids seemed not to notice that Katie slept in the girls' room, forcing Ford to take the master bedroom after she'd realized how restless he was during the night. Unavoidably attuned to his every move, she knew he rarely slept for long and had convinced him that he'd be less likely to wake the kids if he had his own room.

With a shaky, unspoken truce, they busied themselves with a life of sorts. Both of them knew a reckoning had to come—they had to exorcise their demons and see where they stood when the smoke cleared. Neither of them was in any hurry to stir that up.

CHAPTER NINE

HIS BREATH CAME IN ragged gasps, his chest on fire as he struggled for air, falling from the bed to the floor. Ford had never experienced asthma before this last deployment, before there was sand in what seemed like every breath of air, before the world blew up and broke him into pieces. He hadn't had a trauma-induced attack in weeks, not since the last deep nightmare he'd been trapped in. Knowing he just needed to wake up, but being unable to do so fast enough, made things worse, for there was no logic amid the fight for the air he needed to draw a breath.

Pushing up off the floor, Ford's head collided with something, causing him to see even more stars as he came to full consciousness. "Damn it all to hell!" His hands shot up to cradle his throbbing head.

"Here, here. Ford, breathe!" He felt the smooth tip of the inhaler against his mouth, a cool, almost roughly firm hand urging his mouth to close around the contraption that would restore his airway. Fully awake, Ford took the inhaler from Katie's hand, his other hand coming up to squeeze her arm in reassurance that he was awake and dealing with it now. He stood and dropped to sit on the bed's edge, looking up to see Katie rub her jaw where she'd connected with her husband's hard head.

"Oh, man, Katie, did I hurt you? Let me see." His breath still a bit ragged, Ford tossed the inhaler aside and reached for her.

When she drew back from him, he froze with a curse, assuming she was afraid of him at the moment. "I'm sorry," he said softly.

"Ford Callahan, you didn't hurt me—we're too hard headed to be knocking heads, that's all." Katie rolled her eyes at him.

"How did you know?" He gestured to the inhaler lying amid the crumpled sheets.

"I saw it the other day when Scarlett unpacked for you. Why wasn't it within reach, Ford? People die from asthma attacks." Her fear crept through, her voice shaking.

"I haven't needed it for a few weeks—I got lazy about it." Ford scrubbed his hands back and forth through his hair, making it stand on end. Taking deep, full breaths, he stood. "I need to get outside."

"It's three am," Katie said, glancing out the window into the night.

Ford's chuckle was rueful. "Yeah, I'm familiar with three am. We aren't pals, but we do okay."

He pulled on a t-shirt and left the room.

* * *

Katie scooped up the inhaler and dropped it into the pocket of her robe. The house was quiet and dim, lit only by the hall nightlight and the light over the kitchen sink. Assuring herself that the commotion hadn't woken any of the kids, Katie detoured to the kitchen to push the coffee button and take two bottles of water from the fridge. She took a moment to breathe, to calm the terror she'd felt since seeing him fight for air and consciousness amid the nightmare. Katie recalled how she'd again reminded Ford of the B&B by sticking a note with the name and address on his bathroom mirror. What if he did move out and had one of those attacks when he was alone? Her stomach felt full of ice as she imagined him alone, imagined his frantic grappling for the elusive inhaler. But he'd made it all these months without her help, hadn't he? Blowing out a breath, she filled the coffee mugs, her mind racing, her emotions all over the place.

On the porch, she handed him a mug and dropped to the step beside him.

Ford sipped the coffee, letting his breath out with a soft whoosh.

Katie nudged his knee with hers. "How long has that been going on?"

"Awhile. It's not uncommon over there, with the frequent blowing sand as well as the open trash burning. Nasty air most days. The doctor said it would likely go away in time." Ford shrugged slightly, his hands hanging between his knees as he leaned forward, taking measured, deliberate breaths. "I'm sorry I woke you."

"You're—what??" Katie's head whipped around, her expression incensed in the dim light from the string of lights along the porch railing.

"I know how hard it is for you to get back to sleep once you're woken." A slight smile quirked up at the corner of his mouth.

"Ford, you were fighting to breathe. I think that's a good enough reason for me to lose some sleep."

They both fell silent, sipping coffee, looking out into the pre-dawn darkness. The ocean's ever-present rumble, the croaks of ground frogs and hoots of owls combined with the light hibiscus scented breeze to soothe both of them.

*   *   *

Katie looked to the bakery next door. "Reggie will be showing up soon."

"Time to make the doughnuts?" The words out before he'd hardly thought them, Ford nearly sputtered in his coffee at his own joke.

A giggle escaped as Katie did sputter her own sip. "You did *not* just say that."

Ford laughed out loud before Katie reached over and clapped a hand over his mouth.

Swallowing the laugh, Ford soaked up her touch. She wasn't willingly touching him much these days, and definitely not while laughing. Unable to stop himself, he reached up to hold her hand in place over his mouth, pursing his lips against her fingers. She smelled so good, scents that were Katie, in his mind. She'd always been a coffee junkie, a fact that had been clear the moment they'd met when she was barely twenty years old.

He'd literally run into her on the landing of his buddy's apartment building, spilling her coffee everywhere, which resulted in a scathing diatribe from her on his character and carelessness. Completely charmed by her, he'd ended up promising her a cup of said coffee every day for a week if she'd have it with him. From there, they'd tumbled into days of hazy afternoons together, stolen hours in her shabby apartment between her morning and evening shifts and his morning PT and night job.

At the moment, Katie didn't try to pull away, didn't stiffen or scold him yet. Emboldened by that, he made tiny licks across her palm with the tip of his tongue. He set his mug aside and brought his other hand up to hold her small hand in both of his big ones, turning it over and kissing along the backs of her fingers. She drew in a sharp breath and tugged on her hand slightly, but relaxed when he didn't let go. Ford, learning that small victories were a very big deal, kissed her hand once more and went still. Neither of them moved for the space of several heartbeats, the sea breeze sifting through the coconut trees, the whispering sound harmonizing with that of the waves.

Just when he drew a breath to speak, the screen door squeaked lightly.

* * *

"Mommy?" Miriam stood in the doorway, her tawny hair tumbling into her face, a hand rubbing her eyes.

"Right here, little one." Katie turned sideways to lean against the porch railing, holding out her arms for the girl to crawl into her lap.

"Bad dream?" Katie wrapped her arms around her daughter, brushing back the hair from her forehead.

Miri nodded, burying her face in her mother's shoulder.

"Want to talk about it, baby?" Ford rubbed the little back gently.

Miriam shook her head, her face still buried.

Katie met Ford's eyes over their daughter's back, the shared moment with their child between them feeling like so many moments before.

When he leaned in to take Miri in his arms, Katie took the moment to look at him closely, his gaze on their daughter as he talked to her softly. The lines that bracketed his eyes were deep. She'd first thought they were from squinting against the sun while deployed, but in the days since he'd been home, she had noticed he narrowed his eyes often—some days more often than not. Did his head hurt that much?

Making a mental note to ask him about it, Katie leaned her head back against the porch and closed her eyes, letting the deep timbre of Ford's voice lull her as he told Miri about a hot air balloon he'd once seen. Distraction was, after all, a parent's finest tool.

Moments later, the little girl was again asleep, curled into her daddy's chest.

"You know, I dreamed about her one night." His voice was barely a whisper. "So vividly, it scared me that something had happened, but I was in the field and couldn't check in."

Katie inclined her head. "When was that?"

"Hmmm. I think around the first of the year, maybe." His hand rubbed Miri's back as she slept, his chin resting lightly on her head.

"I wonder if that was about the same time she was having nightmares about you?" Katie mused, thinking back. "Right before your accident, she had several nights where she woke up completely freaking out that her daddy was hurt. The first couple of nights I consoled her, put a new picture in her Daddy Bear's pocket, talked about what we'd do when you came home, all the usual things we do when we miss you a lot. After the third time, I tried to call you so she could talk to you, but you'd already gone back out." Tears came to Katie's eyes as she remembered the little girl sobbing, "Somebody help my daddy," over and over as if her heart had broken.

"Poor baby." Ford closed his eyes, kissing Miri's forehead. Holding her close, he stood carefully. "I'll put her back to bed."

Katie stood, too. "Why don't you lie down with her and try to get a few more minutes of sleep? I'm headed to the bakery." Enough remembering things that made her heart ache, not that it ever stopped aching.

His back already to her, Ford nodded, putting out a hand to catch the screen door behind him.

Katie looked at the bakery, the front dark, but the back brightly lit as Reggie set up inside. She finished her coffee as the dark skies began to lighten to gunmetal gray and the lights of the town flickered to life as people began their early mornings.

"Time to make the doughnuts, indeed." She shook her head with a smile.

CHAPTER TEN

"PAPA'S HERE! PAPA'S HERE!" Miriam's dash from where she'd been crouched between Ford's legs while he filled a bird feeder in the back yard nearly toppled her father. In his haste to protect himself from her sudden pop up, Ford dropped the bag of bird seed, spilling most of it on his feet.

"Help me, Daddy!" Scarlett shrieked from the fork in the tree branches where he'd deposited her earlier. Legs kicking, she held out her arms. "I wanna see Papa!"

Obligingly, Ford swung the girl down, smiling at her whoop as she swooshed through the air.

"You know Papa?" Scarlett stopped and turned back to her father.

"I will now," Ford said.

She turned and ran to the house calling, "Papa, Papa!"

Ford shook bird seed from his feet and squatted to scoop some of it back into the bag.

"I believe I see a man in need of a drink." Gabe came out the back door of the house, a cold beer bottle in each hand.

Ford stood and took the offered bottle. "Good to see you."

"I brought Amos to visit. He doesn't drive anymore." Gabe surveyed the three bird feeders. "Keeping busy?"

Ford laughed. "Something like that. Three kids, a wife who doesn't know if she likes me or not, a brand new world out here in the ocean."

Gabe clinked their bottles. "Takes time, this much I know. I've only had Rory a short time—long story, but I didn't know she existed until last year. I had no idea what to do with a kid. All I could do was show up. I suspect what you're dealing with isn't much different, for what it's worth."

Ford took a deep drink. "Worth a lot, actually. I can show up. By the way, I was thinking I'd drop by the bar. Luke said something about darts. I can throw a dart or two."

"You're on. I'll be behind the bar, and I'm always up for darts."

The two men walked around the side of the house to the front porch where what looked to Ford like at least half the island was hanging out.

"DaddyDaddyDaddy, come see Papa!" Miri tugged Ford's hand, pulling him to the porch swing where Katie sat next to an old man who was clearly holding court. But it was Katie that Ford looked at. She took his breath away, smiling and happy sitting on the swing next to Amos. She'd been estranged from her grandfather since she was a baby, but their reconnection had clearly been successful if the look on her face was any indication. It was Amos who'd entreated her to come to the island, offering her this house and the bakery if she wanted to stay. Ford was interested to hear the entire story, for he'd never even heard of Amos over the years. He remembered that Katie had always treasured two tattered letters from her mother, but she'd tucked them away and he'd never seen her read them.

"Here, Ford." Charlie, her riotous curls piled on her head, carried a little boy who was a blur of movement as she stood up from the porch bench, nudging him with her hip. "Sit."

"I'm not booting you from your seat," Ford protested.

"I'm giving this menace to Uncle Gabe and helping the kids get drinks with minimal kitchen damage. So, sit." Charlie pushed past him, holding the wriggling toddler out to the man at the bottom of the porch steps.

Ford laughed at the baby, a moving bundle of drools and smiles, and took the vacated seat.

"So you're the man who's taken care of my Katie these past few years." Amos's voice was strong despite his frail appearance.

"I don't know about that part, but it's good to meet you." Ford reached out and shook the old man's outreached hand.

Amos gripped his hand and met Ford's eyes with an intent gaze. "Thank you for your service, young man. It's good to have you home."

Recognizing a fellow soldier, Ford met the old man's gaze and nodded. "Sir."

"Oh, I'm just Old Amos these days. Piddling at fishing and holding my seat at Gabe's place."

"I expect to see you on that seat today, Amos," Gabe called from the yard where he rolled a ball with the baby he'd been handed.

"What's cooking?" Amos called back.

"As if I know. I just eat it and man the bar." Gabe shrugged, reaching out to catch Zane by his little shirt before he could crawl away.

"Ppsshhtt, Amos, you know all he cares about are the cheeseburgers. I think Jill told me her seafood gumbo was on the specials board today, but I can't swear to it. You know she'll make sure you get whatever suits you." Charlie returned carrying a tray filled with colorful plastic tumblers that Ford noticed was promptly emptied by a mass of kids—and not all of them his.

A dark-haired girl stopped in front of Ford, Miri at her side. "You're Miri's Daddy."

"I am." Ford smiled, resisting the urge to use his thumb to wipe away the red sugar mustache both girls wore.

"She missed you a lot." Serious gray eyes surveyed him.

"I missed her a lot." Ford's arm went around his daughter, who'd moved to sit on his knee.

As if he'd passed some test, the girl then smiled at him, her gap-toothed grin making him grin back.

The two girls dashed off the porch, following Owen and several others around the side of the house, their shrieks and calls a cacophony of riotous noise.

The whole scene both unsettled and pleased Ford. He was glad his family had found friends on the island, but the level of people and noise had him edgy. He unconsciously rolled his shoulders, as if his shirt was too tight. Logically he knew so-called reentry would take adjustment time, but sometimes it was hard to remember why he was feeling that way in the moments when he looked about for an escape route.

"Hey, Ford, help me out here?" Gabe called from the side of the road where his beat-up blue truck was parked. The busy baby was securely strapped into a car seat, throwing all objects within his reach to the floor or out the door.

Relieved for something to do, Ford eased his way through the kids and women on the porch, swinging Scarlett when she grabbed onto his arm, winking when he caught Katie's eye.

"Whew." He blew out a breath and leaned on the truck's open hood. "What's up?"

Across from him, the other man met his gaze. "Nothing. You just looked a little boxed in up there."

Ford winced. "That bad, huh?"

"No, I've just been there. I can imagine combat aftermath is different than a fire aftermath, but I recognize trapped when I see it."

Ford nodded, rubbing the back of his neck.

Gabe closed the truck's hood. "Come on by the bar, let's see your dart skills. I warn you, Owen has bragged. A lot."

Gabe picked up the tossed objects and chucked the slobbery baby chin with a grin as he climbed into the truck. "Amos will need a ride whenever he's ready."

With a wave, Ford stepped back to let Charlie and Rory into the truck.

"Seeya later, Miri's Daddy." Rory hugged his legs, already chattering to the baby as she climbed in.

"Don't forget the brownies for girls' night, Katie!" Charlie teased.

Katie did not forget such things, in fact, she was known for bringing more than one delicious baked treat to their girls' night out gatherings.

Ford watched the truck drive away for a moment before he turned back to the porch.

"Brownies?"

"Girls' night." Katie stuck her tongue out at him, earning herself a return favor.

Owen bragged, huh? "Hey, Owen!"

The boy's head popped out from—under the porch? Ford raised an eyebrow.

Owen's dirt-smeared face grinned, a finger on his lips, his expression begging his father to keep his secret.

Ford rubbed his jaw nonchalantly and walked to the porch steps. "Anybody seen Owen?"

Seconds later, the boy in question popped through the door of the house, sharing a conspiratorial wink with his father.

"Let's go find a dart board, kid." Ford looked at Katie, patting his cargo pockets.

"Just tell Keno to put it on the account. Island life." She waved a hand at the trees and impossibly blue sky.

Island life, indeed.

With the girls occupied elsewhere, father and son set off down the street.

*   *   *

Watching them go, Katie could almost believe things were as they should be. Ford was home, his son by his side, his daughters often dangling from one arm or the other. But, like her, his body—inside and out—bore fresh scars of the past year. They'd weathered hell while apart, how was it possible to still be Katie and Ford when so much had changed? Amos's touch on her hand brought Katie's attention back to him. "He's a good man, I see that. So what's wrong?"

Amos had wasted no time getting to know his granddaughter after being reunited with her. He'd shown her pictures and told her stories and made her feel like she'd known him forever—he certainly had known her forever. She didn't mind that he spoke his mind when it suited him; he meant well.

"Such a gaping chasm between us, you know?" Katie squeezed his hand.

"Then you build a bridge." Amos's faded blue eyes held her gaze fast. "You build a bridge, girl."

CHAPTER ELEVEN

"OOOHH," KATIE GROANED as she slid down into the tub, the water as hot as she could stand it. What a day. It had been worth it, but her neck throbbed mercilessly, her shoulder keeping an accompanying beat. Marathon baking wasn't for the weak, that's for sure. Just as she laid her head back, a soft tap came at the door, and Ford stuck his head in.

Katie went still, watching as his gaze traveled over her body, mostly hidden beneath the steaming bubbles in the room lit only by a small lamp on the shelf. When his eyes reached hers, she forced herself to be nonchalant and lifted a brow. "Need something?"

Ford laughed, the sound low and suggestive. His gaze traveled up and down her again. "Definitely."

"Ford," she admonished, suppressing a smile. What wife didn't enjoy her husband's appreciation, sort of estranged or not? But, in this case, her secret was dangerously close to the surface.

"Cut foot on a small person. That cream you use?" His expression gave away what Katie knew was in his mind's eye— what he knew was under those bubbles. Her chestnut eyes were both amused and irritated, the shadows under them showing her weariness.

She winced a little as she brought her arm up to point at the cabinet. "In there."

"You're hurting?" He took a step closer.

"It'll pass." She dismissed him, closing her eyes.

She heard him take another step closer, but before she could open her eyes, a little voice filled the air.

"Daddy! I need a Hello Kitty band aid, too!" The yell brought them both back to reality like a splash of cold water.

At his sigh, a smile tugged at the corner of her mouth. "Same place."

With a heartfelt yet exaggerated groan, he got the necessary items and closed the door behind him.

Katie sighed, using one finger to turn on the iPod docked on the tub's deep ledge beside her and sinking further into the water. The soft strains of slow jazz filled the dimly lit room, and she let herself imagine what Ford might have done next if he hadn't been summoned by a tiny imperious princess—and if she wasn't keeping an unfair secret from him.

* * *

"Washed, kissed, medicated, bandaged. Mission Accomplished." Ford swooped Scarlett up and kissed her cheeks all over, her giggles making him grin. Carrying her into the girls' room, he snuggled her gently into the bed next to her already sleeping sister. Tucking the lightweight pink and yellow quilt around both of them, he whispered "Sweet dreams, princesses." Scarlett's eyes were already closing, her arms around a doll that looked like her. Seeing both girls' Daddy Bears abandoned at the foot of the bed made him feel good. They clung to the bears when he was downrange and apparently didn't feel the need for them now. The bears sported a tiny copy of his ACU shirt with a clear picture pocket on the front. Before he left every time, Katie would take a picture of him with each child and they'd put it in the pocket. When they missed him particularly strongly, Katie would pull out a box of pictures for them to sift through and pick another one for the pocket. The ritual of sifting through pictures and talking about him seemed to help—at least for a time. To the tune of his girls' soft, snuffly snores, Ford left the room, pulling the door half-closed behind him.

A peek into Owen's room showed the boy sprawled in his hammock, a book face down against his cheek. The sight made Ford smile as he set the book on the night table. He noticed the book was a childhood favorite of his and made a mental note to ask Owen how he was liking it so far. Pulling the blue and green quilt lightly over the boy's legs, he took care to leave Owen's feet bare. His son took after Katie in that he hated his feet covered, ever. That lesson had taken awhile to learn as young parents with a fussy baby—how were they supposed to know a tiny infant wanted his feet out? Ford shook his head slightly at the memory and turned off the lamp.

He paused in the circular hallway, switching on the night lamp on the small table. The little rituals of settling a home down for the night were a comfort. His shoulders relaxed in the dim light as he listened to the sleeping murmurs of his children amid the odd noises from the lizard as he—or was it she?—played in the dark, the low hum of the refrigerator, a distant bicycle bell.

Drawn by an invisible thread, Ford went into the master bedroom and paused in front of the bathroom door. He heard the soft jazz and a soft sloshing of the bath water. She was still in there. Opening the door slowly, he feasted his eyes on the vision his wife made, her eyes widened, her lips parted slightly. Stepping inside the steamy room, he closed the door behind him.

She brought her hands up to her chest. "Ford."

He cleared his throat lightly. "I thought you could use help washing your hair, what with your soreness."

Without waiting for her answer, he knelt by the tub's side and reached to take out the clips that held her hair up. The pile of soft, silky strands in his hands, he leaned in close, breathing in her scent, dropping his head to brush his lips across her forehead, down her cheek.

She shivered slightly, his breath tickling her ear.

He sat back on his heels, the silky dark tresses spilling over his hands like melting chocolate. As the music played, the notes dancing in the steamy air, Ford cupped water in his hands and began to wash her hair. "The first time I helped you wash your hair was the single most intoxicating moment of my life up until then. I've..." His voice gone husky, he cleared his throat. "I'd never experienced a feeling quite like that before."

Leaning her head back into her husband's gentle hands, Katie murmured in agreement, "I remember. I'd never felt so cherished." A soft moan slipped from her as he massaged behind her ears, soapy strands sliding through his fingers.

"It was the day I came home on leave during my first deployment. Owen was two days old. You were barely standing." He reached around to cup her chin, tip her head back so he could rinse the shampoo, using a cup from the tub's ledge. "The reprieve lasted just long enough for me to wash your hair and help you out of the tub. Literally." He chuckled, bringing his hands back to rinse her hair, smoothing the soap bubbles from it. "Your foot touched the floor and Owen cried out." His fingers stroked her jaw, blazing a path of heat down her neck, twirling through the tiny pool of soapy water at the notch in her collarbone, catching on her shooting star pendant. "When did you get this?"

Katie took the pendant from him with a slight shrug. "A while back."

Her shoulders hunched, she caught her lip between her teeth, spurring Ford to pick up the memory again in hopes of relaxing her.

"Those days are hazy, but I remember my shock at suddenly having a wife and newborn son. I couldn't believe this orphan boy had gotten so lucky twice." Both of them fell silent, lost in remembering. Finished with her hair, Ford sat back on his heels, his hands hanging over the edge of the tub beside her.

"That seems so long ago, yet yesterday," Katie sighed.

He nodded, stroking her arm with a finger, his eyes on her soap-dotted breasts, pebbled against cool air. He dragged in a breath and, bringing his gaze to hers, he whispered, "I promise I will cherish you like that again, if you'll let me."

She looked at him, her eyes soft with memory, wet lashes dark against her tawny sunkissed skin.

He leaned forward, resting his forehead against hers a moment before he pushed to his feet. "I'm going to leave this room right now, because this feeling? I want you to remember it, to hold it close. This is us."

"Ford—"

He turned back and made an exaggerated bow, eyebrow raised. "And now, m'lady, I seek a cold shower."

She covered her mouth on a giggle and with that he did leave the room, leaving her as he'd intended—soft and wanting, filled with memories of the world they'd built together. The world she was certain they could not save, despite his promises.

**CHAPTER TWELVE **

"HEY. C'MON IN, FORD." Gabe turned from readying the bar for the day to find the other man standing in the open doorway.

"I know you're not open yet, but I'm hoping you have a minute." Ford, clearly fresh from a run, crossed the empty room.

Waving the other man over, Gabe filled a glass with ice and water then turned to the coffee station behind him, raising a mug in question.

"Sure." Ford drained the water and leaned on the bar.

Setting filled coffee mugs on the bar, Gabe followed suit, leaning. He watched Ford sip the coffee, waiting. Bartenders as a breed were a patient sort and Gabe himself was even more so.

"I didn't expect to find you here this early. I heard sounds as I ran by and thought I'd check it out."

Okay, small talk it is. Gabe's mouth twisted wryly. "There are six little girls in my cottage." For added emphasis, he tapped the bar with a finger with each word, "Six giggly, hungry, silly, adorable girls."

Ford laughed. "Ah, yes. Your only recourse being escape—as long as adequate reinforcements for your wife have been obtained." Miriam had been so excited for Rory's birthday sleepover, he could only imagine her times five.

Gabe raised his mug in salute, "Thank goodness for Reggie and Jill."

Ford returned the salute.

"How's island life suiting you thus far, Ford?"

"Island life is...well, it's good. Different." Ford gave a slight shrug.

Gabe nodded, "I came here seeking a slower pace, desperate to get away from the noise. I had no idea what I was getting into." He gave a short laugh.

"Yeah, I know the pace of normal life outside of a war zone is very different, but island time is even more different." Ford sipped coffee, settling on a bar stool with a sigh.

"Too slow?" A grin tugged at the corner of Gabe's mouth. Ford was far from the first person to be incredulous that island life on island time really did exist as more than a vacation. That people actually lived such a slow pace day in and day out.

"I don't know that I need a full time job, just yet, but...something." Ford dragged a hand through his sweat-dampened hair.

"Tell you what, why don't you start fishing with us when we go out—usually four out of seven days...ish." Gabe laughed at Ford's predictable grimace. Military types didn't embrace the 'ish' of island time easily.

"That'll give you some routine for those mornings. Nash and I'll actually teach you the ropes, then we'd have backup instead of canceling on those mornings one of us can't make it. We started this gig before either of us had kids, when we didn't need backup."

"Good idea," Ford said thoughtfully.

"You know what else I just thought of? We have a three-person First Responder squad that might could use your med evac experience. With the lead in experience and helo backup pilot being Luke, it makes for a juggling act as sheriff some days. Neither that nor fishing would have to be full time, but it'd give you plenty to do around the kids and Katie. Go by and see Luke about it. Once over the bridge, first street on the right, you'll see the station."

Ford found his hands suddenly jumpy at the thought of a helo stick under them again. He sighed, knowing that wasn't going to happen.

"I can't fly—post-concussive issues—but I can do the rest. And Katie doesn't know that 'can't fly' part yet, okay?" Ford stood and stretched gingerly. He'd run harder this morning, trying to shake off a noisy head night.

"Secret's safe with me. Plenty of other things you can do," Gabe replied, gathering up their coffee cups as Ford called out his thanks and loped out onto the sand.

Gabe watched him go, knowing a good man when he saw one. Thanks to Charlie, and to Ford's comments on the boat the other day, he knew that things were rough between Ford and Katie right now.

A while back, Charlie had told him Katie had admitted to it being the toughest deployment they'd faced in ten years of military life and that she was unsure of the long term effects on their marriage. Not usually one to spill girls' night secrets to Gabe, Charlie had confided in him when she recruited him to help in forming a circle of people she hoped would become a tribe, a family for Katie and the kids. Gabe smiled at the thought of his warm, generous wife. How he'd gotten so lucky, he'd never know.

Now to to give Luke a quick heads up call. The other man would be pleased. Ford might need the activity, but the First Responders certainly could use his expertise.

CHAPTER THIRTEEN

UPON HIS RETURN from the run and talking with Gabe, Ford found Katie in the porch hammock cradling Miri, the little girl sobbing as if her heart was broken. Alarmed, Ford's gaze flew to his wife's. Her expression eased back his reaction. While there was clearly a problem, there was no emergency.

"Hey, Miribelle, I thought you were at Rory's party." Ford squatted next to the hammock, gently wiping Miri's face with the edge of her blanket. With fresh sobs, she shook her head and threw herself into his arms.

Ford sat down hard, arms catching their daughter against him.

"Want to tell me what's wrong?" His voice was soft against Miri's ear, his hands rubbing her back slowly.

The girl shook her head, hitching sobs slowing.

"Can Mommy tell me why you're not at the sleepover?"

This time Miri nodded, keeping her face buried against him.

"She woke up scared for you. Jill brought her home," Katie said, reaching out to smooth damp tendrils from the child's face.

"I'm here, Miribelle, I'm not going anywhere." Ford closed his eyes as fresh sobs shook Miri's body, each one a jab to his heart.

"But y—your job is saving soldiers who get h-hurt. You have to go back." Miri's tear-filled blue eyes met his own. It never failed to move him to see his own eyes looking back at him from this child's face.

"I'm done with that job now. And like any other job, baby, there are lots of good pilots to take my place."

"You don't have to go to work anymore?"

"I'm not going anywhere, Miriam Mary Callahan. I promise." Testing the porch railing with one hand, Ford scooted back to lean against it, arms snug around her, humming 'You Are My Sunshine.' Sobs faded into hiccups, then soft sighs as she drifted off to sleep. Ford continued to rock slightly, humming slower and softer.

"Why didn't you call me?" He looked at Katie, an accusing note in his voice.

"Honestly, Ford, it didn't occur to me in the moment." Katie crossed her arms, chin raised.

Ford nodded, accepting that he'd earned that, but feeling the sharp sting nonetheless.

They sat wordlessly for awhile, their daughter's hitching sighs and soft snuffles joining the early morning island sounds. Katie pushed the hammock with her foot, setting it to swaying slightly.

"Has it been this hard for her often?" Ford's chin rested atop Miri's head, his arms still wrapped around her.

Katie nodded. "Somewhat. Especially since June." She cleared her throat, resting her forehead in her hands. "Even though I didn't tell them you'd been hurt for quite a while, she started crying for you most nights."

"And once I started calling again?"

"It got better. She'd still wake up crying, but then I'd set up Skype or a text, and she'd be fine."

Ford held Miri securely and pushed to his feet. "Let me get her into bed."

Katie nodded, following him inside to make coffee. She heard him moving about in the girls' room, then shortly after that the shower came on.

Katie took her mug and slipped out the door. Inside the bakery, she flipped on lights and turned oven knobs, breathing a sigh of relief. It was here that things were predictable, and that brought her no small amount of satisfaction every day. Here, in the hours before anyone else was around, she could think about the secret she kept deep in her heart. The secret she knew would send Ford reeling and likely obliterate any chances they had at a future.

CHAPTER FOURTEEN

LUKE HUNG HIS HANDS on the top of the door frame to stretch fully in hopes of unkinking his back after the mostly useless quick afternoon nap he'd snatched on the cot in the First Responder station. The small station matched the island in size, but boasted a kick-ass staff and top notch equipment enabling them and the island's small hospital to avoid air evacuations to the bigger islands whenever possible. Kick-ass notwithstanding, Luke pulled double, sometimes triple, duty as sheriff, EMT and backup chopper pilot. While most of the time the team could handle things, the last few days he'd been needed in some way or other nearly round the clock. Listening to the man standing in front of the dispatcher right now brought Luke a flash of hope that he might have a few hours free now and then to pursue a certain sexy bar manager/waitress. He and Jane had been flirting hard for several weeks now, but neither had made any significant moves. Luke was hesitant to woo the lady when it seemed he rarely slept in his own bed or ate at his own—or any other—table these days.

Tuning back into the conversation at hand, Luke let go of the door frame and stepped into the front office. "You're on, Ford."

Ford had been explaining his desire to help out the squad to Ruthie, the current dispatcher, a friendly, self-proclaimed honorary aunt and matchmaker extraordinaire to all.

At Luke's comment, Ruthie clipped pages to a clipboard and handed it to Ford. "Give us your contact info for your phone. We'll give you a radio, too, since cell service can be flaky. And welcome aboard."

"How often you want to be on, Ford?" Luke already knew much about Ford's capabilities between time spent with Katie and the kids and his friendship with Gabe and Nash. While Katie didn't talk about Ford much, there was Owen and his pride in his father.

Ford shook the other man's outstretched hand. "What do you need?"

"Another EMT mainly. We handle things pretty well until somebody needs all three of me at the same time in different places." Luke grinned. He loved the island and loved his job, just hoped for some breathing room now and then. "How about you tune in to the radio and join us on some calls for a few days? Get a feel for things." Luke handed Ford a walkie-talkie-style radio and went to the supply closet."Let's go up in the helo tomorrow morning, scope out the island, orient you in general. No better way to see it all than bird's eye view."

"Sounds like a plan." Ford took the box of gear that included a portable siren for his Jeep, a vest with bright reflective strips and a utility belt.

Leaving the station, Ford hoped Katie would see his joining the squad for what it was, a need to be busy doing something rather than a need to pull away or a longing for the helo stick.

CHAPTER FIFTEEN

ALMOST LIKE WHEN Ford was deployed, Katie waited for the other shoe to drop. She knew him, she knew his hands had to be itching for his helo stick despite his insistence that he was done. They had been a full-time military family for so long, she couldn't imagine that Ford wouldn't be at least planning for his next deployment anytime now. Assuming his time with them was stretching out due to time needed to be sure he was healed, she found herself thinking about what she'd say when he came to tell her he was leaving again. This time, she and the kids would not be moving to wherever he'd be calling home base, they'd be staying here on the island. Katie told herself she wasn't like those military spouses who said they were all in, but couldn't truly be there for their soldiers and folded when things got tougher. This was different. He'd started the rift, and she'd responded the only way she knew to protect herself.

Setting a timer for the bread dough working in the big mixer, Katie moved to set up a frosting station to work on cookies next. The back door opened behind her, the booted footsteps alerting her to Ford's arrival. She continued to work, but felt the hairs on the back of her neck prickle as he walked closer.

A big hand reached over her shoulder and stole a cookie, the heat of his body giving her the urge to lean back against him.

"Cookie thief."

"Shameless." Ford moved to lean back against the long counter, watching her efficiently frost cookie after cookie, her work nearly flawless every time. "I never heard you mention a bakery. Is it something you thought about a lot?"

Katie shook her head, the tip of her tongue caught between her teeth in concentration. Three more cookies frosted and set aside, she unsuccessfully tried to toss an errant strand of hair from her face by tossing her head then wiping her cheek on her shoulder. Ford chuckled and reached over to tuck away the wayward strand, his thumb and forefinger lingering along the shell of her ear a moment.

Katie shivered involuntarily at his touch, moving away. "No, it's not something I thought about at all until I came here."

During Ford's first deployment, when she was pregnant with Owen, Katie had set herself to learning how to bake bread and cookies, then cakes followed by pies. She thought back to that time, a time when she was living alone yet not alone at all. For the first time in her life since the loss of her parents at a young age, she'd had enough grocery money to spend on baking supplies and, for a girl who'd lived on less than nothing for so long, baking her own bread and cookies was nourishing to body and soul.

Wiping her hands on her apron, Katie arched her back in a stretch and turned to the coffee maker. "After I found Amos and visited here that first time, the bakery owner at the time mentioned how he wasn't sure how Amos would take it when he told him he was leaving, thus leaving nobody to run the bakery his wife—my grandmother—had loved so much. The idea of taking this place over didn't occur to me until—" She poured them both cups of coffee, a sigh escaping as she continued, "Until things went to hell and I needed to get away."

"Pretty good getaway, edge of the world," Ford remarked, reaching to steal another cookie.

"The perfect match." He gestured to his coffee cup with the cookie.

Katie helped herself to a cookie, making little sound of appreciation as she nibbled. "Mmmm, my favorite—this week."

Ford went still, watching her lips as she ate the cookie, his body tightening in response.

Clearing his throat, he said, "So, I have news."

Here it is, Katie thought. This is why what I would say when he tells me he's got to go was on my mind today.

"Oh?" She forced herself to look up from her coffee and meet his eyes. Today the blue was laser sharp and clear. She gripped her cup tighter, the act keeping her from reaching up to smooth the lines beside those eyes, to soothe the throb she knew resided there.

"I got a job today," he said.

"You already have a job. World's Number One Flying Ace," she said, her tone light as she turned away to wash her hands and resume cookie detail. She couldn't look at him while he told her he was leaving again soon.

"Well, yeah, this factors that in."

"Okay." She drew out the word, tossing him a glare for the stalling.

"Gabe told me the island's First Responders could use another team member, especially one with my experience."

Katie lifted an eyebrow and pursed her lips. "Good idea, Gabe."

"Yeah? I thought so, as did Luke. I'm in, got some gear and orientation plans for the next few days." He leaned against the counter.

Finishing up the cookies, Katie moved to the dough mixer to set the loaves up.

"Well?" he asked.

"Well, what?" she replied.

"Seriously?" Ford rolled his eyes.

Katie laughed, her hands expertly shaping the dough into loaves that would go in the proofer to rise and be ready to bake by morning.

Strolling back over to her side, Ford stuck out a finger menacingly.

"Do not poke my dough, Ford Callahan." Katie elbowed him, hard. "It's not rising yet, but you'll get germs in it."

Loaves finished, Katie gathered various utensils to carry to the sink. Ford took them from her while she gathered more. "All done but the washing up. The job is a great idea, I think, Ford. As long as you feel up to it. I wondered how long you'd be able to hang loose— 'tisn't really your style."

Ford placed the utensils in the sink and turned on the hot water. "A world where 'ish' is a valid measure of time gives me pause, I'll admit." His grimace was cute, she couldn't help but notice.

Katie laughed, "Putting it mildly, I'm sure."

They made short work of the dishes, Katie telling him to leave them to air dry on the draining board when he offered to dry for her. "Grab that white box right there and load it with cookies. We'll take some with us to the beach."

The kids were with Reggie for The Painted Parrot S'mores Night on the beach with both local and tourist kids. Offering Kids' Nights had been one of Charlie's contributions to the amenities and offerings at The Painted Parrot Cove, Gabe's high-end rental properties.

Before she could spin away from him again, Ford caught Katie's hand in his, tugging her close.

"I really, really miss you," he whispered against her ear, his breath tickling her, giving her goosebumps.

"If you could only understand the peace I feel when I'm near you—everything else fades away."

Katie brought her hands up to his chest where Ford captured them and dropped his head to her shoulder.

His hair was soft against her cheek, his beard stubble arousingly prickly against her neck.

Ford squeezed her hands. "Are we ever going to be able to truly talk?" His whisper was hoarse and hesitant.

Just then Katie's phone chimed her ringtone for Owen. Relieved, she moved away from him to pick up the phone. She laughed, showing Ford the text, the tense moment broken.

Are you bringing Dad and cookies?

They both laughed, moving to load the cookie boxes quickly.

"That we can do," Ford said.

Katie texted the boy back, tied the boxes together and put them in Ford's outstretched hands. Glancing around the room, she gestured for Ford to go ahead out the back door, flipping off the bakery lights behind her.

Just like that, life moved on—moment by moment.

CHAPTER SIXTEEN

THE CHASM THAT FAIRLY SCREAMED with echoes between him and Katie, plus the lateness of the hour, made Ford more than a little surprised to look up from where he sprawled on the bed with his laptop to find her standing in the open doorway of the bedroom.

His heart did a slow roll at the tiredness etched on her face. "Can't sleep?"

She shrugged half-heartedly, a tea tag dangling from the mug she cradled in her hand. "Hard to wind down, like the kids, I guess."

"Want me to tell you a bedtime story?" He waggled his eyebrows and patted the bed beside him.

He was rewarded with an eye roll and a smile, further surprised when she joined him on the bed.

"What're you doing?" she asked.

Encouraged that she'd sought out his company in the night, Ford turned his laptop towards her, keeping his hand over the screen. "These were taken the day of. I warn you, they're tough to see."

Several of Ford's unit had been keeping in touch with him via email. Today he'd had opened his new messages to find pictures of himself and his crew with the helicopter they'd fondly called Ford's Mistress. In fact, these pictures had been taken minutes before he'd swung into the cockpit to fly what would turn out to be his last mission for the Army—and his last time manning a helo stick.

Ford licked his lips, rubbing a hand across his stubbled jaw, the raspy sound loud in the quiet room. "Okay?"

Katie nodded, chewing her bottom lip, eyes on the screen.

Turning the computer halfway back around, Ford's finger touched the man in front of him in the picture and slid across four faces. "These didn't make it out." His eyes traveled back and forth over the faces of his men. Men he'd laughed with, fought beside and even fought with, men he'd hated, men he'd loved, all men he'd sworn to die with—die for.

Katie moved up to sit beside him, setting her tea aside. She traced his picture with her fingers, his arm hooked around the helo's frame, his body half in and half out of the cockpit. She tapped his intent, sunglass-shielded face. "Game face," she whispered.

The next picture was a brutal, harshly lit field hospital scene. The patient's head, torso and left leg were wrapped in blood soaked bandages, tubes snaked from multiple angles, clothing in shreds where it'd been torn or cut away. A white-knuckled hand gripped the inside arm of another soldier, the blood-splattered forearm muscles corded and standing out in stark detail. The standing soldier leaned close, grasping the injured soldier's arm, his uniformed shoulder blocking a clear view.

Even with all that, it took Katie only a few seconds to recognize Ford's body on that gurney. Her gasp was swift and sharp, her hand shooting out to clench his thigh.

Ford started to close the laptop but was stopped by her reaching out to scroll to the next picture. This one was clearly taken later, in better conditions on all fronts. The bandages were smaller and snowy white, the dirt and grime washed away, the bruises colorful but fading. Ford's steely blue eyes were slightly unfocused, bracketed by pain creases as he sported a thumbs up for the camera. A laughing woman leaned close in the photo, kissing his cheek, obviously holding a phone out to take the picture.

Before Katie could ask, he cleared his throat and spoke. "Jackie, the wife of my buddy, Trevor. At the time, she said to send it to you, to show you I earned my keep. She was teasing, but she really wanted you to know I was going to be okay."

"I would have liked that." Katie touched the image of his face, her fingers caressing the bruises, the white bandage that covered the wound that was now what the kids called his Harry Potter scar.

Ford closed his eyes, suddenly finding it hard to draw a decent breath. "I need air. Come out to the porch with me?" He was loath to break the moment with his wife, but the walls were closing in on him. He didn't wait for her answer, his chest tightening as the memories of that horrific day played afresh in his head. Getting out into the open air was his single-minded focus.

He stood at the bottom of the porch steps, hands clasped behind his head as he looked up at the stars visible at the edges of the wide coconut tree leaves. Drawing deep breath after deep breath, he calmed his galloping heart, the sheen of fine sweat drying in the night air. On one hand, he wanted to take off for a run next to the sea, let the pounding of his feet on the tide-packed sand coupled with loud music in his ears drown out the sounds of screams and explosions in his head. Let the tang of the saltwater-laden air soothe his sand roughened lungs. Running also let him believe his body truly worked again after so long. But in this moment, he also wanted to cling to Katie, for she was what he'd longed for every minute of every day.

*   *   *

Unsure if she should touch him, Katie pocketed her phone as she came to Ford's side. Arms crossed, a hand at her throat, she spoke quietly, "Let's beach walk?" Somehow, in this moment, her anger was nowhere to be found. Her secret did still burn deep inside, but— for once—it wasn't the center of her attention.

Before Ford could reply, Reggie's bike popped around the corner of the bakery, the light bright in the dimly lit street, the bells jingling in the night's quiet. Parking the bike in front of the bakery, Reggie took a backpack from the basket and gave them a wave as she stepped lightly up the cottage steps and slipped inside.

"It's a great couch." Katie shrugged at Ford's questioning look. Thankful for friends who responded to a text in the wee hours, she held out her hand to him.

With that, he took her outstretched hand, and they walked across the park to the darkened beach, lit only by the light from a quarter moon reflecting off the sea and sand.

"It's always easy to see the stars out here," Katie said, reveling in the feel of his big hand engulfing her smaller one. She'd always loved his hands. They were—or had been—one of those couples who held hands more often than not.

Leaving shoes at the edge of where the park ended and the beach began, they strolled down to the water's edge and turned to walk up the beach. Behind them, The Painted Parrot was dark and quiet, the iconic multicolored lights always lit and swaying in the breeze. Neither spoke for awhile, both absorbing the peace.

"We were blindsided—but isn't everybody over there?" Ford said, his head still noisy with the day of the incident that left him nearly dead.

Katie tightened her hold on his hand.

"The first thing I remember after the explosion is the dead silence. In the dark, I could see smoke and flames all around, people running, bodies everywhere. Suddenly Trevor was there, pulling a woman off me, obviously yelling for help. I couldn't hear a single sound. It was so spooky." Ford rubbed his jaw, his hand coming to rest at his throat.

Katie walked away from the water's edge a few feet and sat down, tugging him along with her. She pulled off her t-shirt—the tank she wore underneath enough for the warm island night—and spread it on the sand. She lay back, her head on the shirt, and patted the space next to her.

Loving that she knew him so well, knew how comforting the stars were for him, Ford lay back on the sand and let his eyes drift over the heavens.

"When Trevor came to me, he took one look and pushed me to lie back. I remember the stars so clearly. Just before I passed out, I hoped you and the kids would always remember to look at the stars, even without me."

"We would have, but I'm glad you're here to share in it. They'd be lost without you," Katie replied, her body resting against his.

"What about you, Katiebean?" he asked, his fingers caressing her arm.

"I'm glad you're alive, Ford," she said simply.

They lay in silence for a while, lulled by twinkling stars above them and the ebb and flow of the waves at their feet.

"I just wish you would have come home to me, or let us stay close by with you." Her words were barely audible above the waves.

"I truly thought I was doing what was best." Ford turned to face her, desperate for her to understand.

Katie sat up. "On what planet would I not want you home, no matter what, Ford?" Frustrated at the ever-present wall between them, she pushed to her feet to pace the sand.

Ford sat up, wrapping his arms around his knees.

"Ten years of watching you go off to war. Ten years of chanting in my head every hour of every day, of watching the door for you to come back to me. By all that is holy, *how* could you think you'd be a burden to your own wife, in your own home?" She stopped in front of him, kicking sand at his legs.

Ford lifted his hands and let them fall, his gaze meeting hers in the moonlight. "You didn't need a husband who could only writhe in his own agony or pass out with the help of drugs or booze."

Katie voiced her frustration with a loud groan, marching up the beach a few steps before rounding on him again. "You know the worst part of it all? Knowing you didn't feel like I could handle helping you made *me* feel like a burden, Ford. A duty instead of a partner. Like you'd just been doing the right thing in taking care of me from the minute I got pregnant."

With that, Katie turned on her heel and headed back down the beach. There it was. The anger that sustained her. She stalked all the way home and closed herself in the bakery for the rest of the night.

CHAPTER SEVENTEEN

"MAN, I NEED A BEER, a shower, food and a bed—in any order after food," Luke groaned, leaning on the door of his sheriff truck as the small crowd around them began to disperse.

"I'm not sure I can move." Tag echoed Luke's groan from his position on the ground, where he downed a second bottle of water. A local who'd lived on the island most of his life, Tag was Luke's right hand man both as a deputy and in rescue.

Vigorously rubbing a towel over his face, Ford grunted agreement, still too winded to speak.

The squad watched the island helicopter fade into the distance, headed for the mainland hospital with the teenagers they'd just spent the last few hours rescuing. A rock tumble in one of the many shallow caves on the island had trapped the pair in rising water, the rescuers breaking through just as more rock tumbled and water rushed in. With his safety line stretched taut and Luke shouting increasingly urgent warnings, Ford had managed to get to the girl as rocks continued to fall and the sea swept her young boyfriend right out the fresh hole. Her terrified screams and flails had been tempered only by Ford crushing her to him, speaking calmly and firmly into her ear, "They will find him, out there. But, Chrissy, we will die right here if you don't let me do my job." His words had sunk in and, still sobbing, the girl had allowed him to strap her to his harness and begin the harrowing backtrack out of the cave.

Thankfully, the boy was saved from being swept out to sea by the two First Responders-a local named Tag and Luke-in the water outside the cave. Unconscious and banged up, he had been taken to shore just as the helicopter arrived.

As the onlookers that had gathered on the shore moved away, Luke reached out a hand to pull Tag to his feet. Matteo called out from the dispersing knot of volunteers to see if they needed anything further, waving back at Luke's answering wave off before he sped off, his dune buggy sending clouds of sand up in its wake.

The trio of rescuers wearily loaded their gear and themselves into the truck, Luke muttering about stupidity and danger.

"Horny kids don't think about rock tumbles and tides, my man. Especially tourists." Ford reached for the sky, his body stretching and popping. It felt so good to be active and alive, his blood pumping, heart pounding. He'd take a harrowing water-filled cave rescue over exploding into pieces on scorching sand any day.

The radio crackled to life as Luke tossed a heavy box from the truck bed into the back seat.

Hearing the details of the call, he jumped into the driver's seat, slammed the truck into gear and bounced up the rocks onto the road.

"On our way, Ruthie." Tag picked up the mic and responded to the call of hikers needing assistance up on the mountain. From the report, all in the trio were conscious and responsive on the phone, bruised and lost with one likely sporting a broken leg.

"No rest for the wicked," Luke shouted, shaking water from his hair and slamming the truck into gear.

"What is this, they all wanna see our handsome faces today?" Ford complained, this being the third straight call with barely a breath between.

"Let's just hope these don't need airlift since our only helo just flew off," Luke said, his jaw jumping as he drove the truck hard. He had lost people simply because giving it their all on the island hadn't been enough and the helicopter hadn't made it in time. It was a risk taken living so far out on the edge of the world, so to speak.

"We really need a designated med evac helo out here, damn it. Then Phil and that bucket he flies can be backup." Ford grumbled the familiar refrain as he assessed his gear bag, restocking it from the box on the seat behind him.

"Preach." Tag thumped Ford's back as he repacked his own gear with practiced efficiency despite the truck's bouncing up the mountain side.

Despite the lamenting about the tough day and throbbing body parts, all three were intently focused on the task ahead as the truck rounded a bend to find the hikers sitting in the middle of the road.

Ford and Tag swung out of the truck before it had barely stopped. Looked like just another day in paradise.

CHAPTER EIGHTEEN

MIRI MELTDOWN. I've got her at the bar.

The text from Gabe sent Ford into overdrive. Still wet from the shower, he wiped his hand on a towel and replied,

On my way.

Tugging on cargo shorts and a t-shirt, damp skin sticking to the clothes, Ford hastily tied on his running shoes and took off on foot.

As he ran, he squinted against the sun—cursing at having left his shades behind. He'd been home alone between calls, hoping a shower followed by going motionless in the dim, cool bedroom would help hold off the looming headache event that had been growing by the hour. It didn't appear to be his lucky day, especially with the sun sending blinding spears of light and heat into his brain. Praying he'd remain upright and functional, Ford slowed to a fast walk as he approached The Painted Parrot.

"Ford!" Gabe called out from the shade of a coconut tree at the edge of the bar's outdoor seating area. Ford was relieved to see his daughter safely on the other man's lap, Gabe's arm around her.

"Hey, Miribelle." Ford said, collapsing into an empty chair next to Gabe. Miri, her face streaked with tears, breath coming in gasping sobs, flung herself into Ford's arms and cried harder.

The searing pain in his head made Ford wince and screw his eyes shut as he wrapped his arms around the girl, murmuring reassurances into her ear.

Taking in Ford's tightly shut eyes and ghostly pallor, Gabe strode into the bar. Back in moments, he draped a cool, damp towel around Ford's neck and pressed a glass of water into his hand.

Ford, eyes still closed, nodded his thanks and drained the glass. In her father's arms, Miri had calmed down, wiping her cheeks. Ford opened one eye a crack and pointed at Gabe's head.

Puzzled, Gabe looked behind him.

"Shades," Ford ground out.

"Ah." Gabe pulled the aviators from his head and handed them over. Slapping them to his face, Ford breathed a sigh of relief, turning his shaded gaze to his hiccupping daughter.

"What happened, baby?"

Miri made a small distressed sound and buried her face again.

Gabe stroked the little girl's sweat-dampened hair back from her tear-streaked face. "Want me to tell him?"

Miri nodded, pressing closer to her father, her sobs finally fading to sniffles and hiccups.

"They were on the beach with Reggie and Tag, he was telling them about his job when his radio went off. She heard you were in the water and when Tag dashed off to help out, she got a little scared is all."

With one finger, Ford tipped Miri's face up. With a strangled curse at her wide, terrified eyes, he pushed the shades to the top of his head so she could see him clearly. Squinting against the waves of sound and light pounding a cacophony of orange and black flashes into his skull, Ford met the blue eyes so like his own. "I'm okay, baby, see?"

"What happened?" Katie ran up to them, breathless, her ponytail coming apart around her face.

Miri stayed in her daddy's arms as Gabe repeated what he'd told Ford.

"Oh, baby." Katie knelt in front of the girl. "I get scared, too, but we know Daddy knows his stuff, right?"

Miri nodded, her breathing returning close to normal, her tears stopped. She clutched Ford's shirt in her hand. Katie smiled, kissing her daughter's forehead. "Want to go to the bakery with me?"

Miri shook her head and pointed down the beach where Reggie and the kids still played.

"Okay, go play. Daddy is done for the day, he'll be close by." With the uncanny resilience of kids, Miri hugged Ford's neck tightly and ran to join her friends again.

Ford stood, fumbling for the shades, his breath hissing out harshly. Gabe pushed another glass of water into his hand. "Drink." Returning Reggie's acknowledging wave as Miri rejoined her friends, Katie turned and got a good look at Ford for the first time. "Mother of God, Ford, what is it?" She'd never seen him pale and shaking like this.

Ford sucked in a deep breath, willing himself not to pass out. "Fuck," he muttered, losing the battle and crumpling to the ground.

* * *

Ford turned his head and opened his eyes cautiously, one at a time. He blew out a breath of relief to find that the crashing of colors and sound that had been roaring about in his skull had downgraded to a mere echo. Sprawled face down, wearing only a pair of running shorts, the room cool and dim, Ford figured Gabe must have realized what was going on and guided Katie in what to do, as he remembered nothing after Miri had run off to play. His post-concussive migraine attacks ranged from annoying flickers to full-on beastly takedowns like this one. Sitting up carefully, pleased to feel no dizziness—they must have poked his meds down him at some point—he then stood and headed for the kitchen, pulling on a t-shirt as he went. He was ravenous.

Katie stood at the counter, sandwich fixings scattered in front of her.

"Either I have excellent timing, or you're a mind reader," Ford said, easing onto a seat at the counter.

"Let's go with both." Katie continued putting together two sandwiches, looking him over with what he'd always called her 'mom doctor assessment' look. "You okay?"

He nodded, then sat bolt upright. "Oh, God—Miri?"

Katie reached out to grasp his arm. "She didn't see. They had moved on down the beach by the time you went down, and Gabe kept the scene low key. He called Luke with his truck—no sirens— and they got you checked out and home."

Ford blew out a sigh of relief. "We'd never get her calmed down again if she'd seen me fall."

Katie widened her eyes in agreement. "No kidding." Pushing a plate to him, she pulled up a bar stool across from him.

"I was terrified until Gabe said he was pretty sure about what was happening after you'd stolen his shades." She smiled slightly. "You're special, by the way, 'cause only Zane steals the Captain's shades."

Ford chuckled, too busy eating to reply.

"I've never seen you look so pale, not even in the hospital."

Swallowing his bite, Ford touched her hand, "I'm sorry I scared you. That's one reason I stayed away to recuperate. It was much worse. I would have terrified all of you on a daily basis."

*   *   *

Katie drew her hand away, her lips pressed together tightly. She busied herself putting away the food and wiping down the counter, reminding herself that anger at him for that didn't help anything. Not to mention if—no, when—he learned her secret, it would be his anger that was justified.

"I don't feel much soreness from falling. I had a black eye and busted lip last time," Ford commented, rolling his shoulders.

"Gabe moved like lightning to break your fall—he lowered you down," Katie answered tersely. "If you're okay alone, I'm going to the bakery. The kids are accounted for, all you have to do is rest." Gabe had assured her that Ford would likely suffer no ill effects he couldn't handle for himself and wouldn't need to be watched once he was awake and alert. Gabe had offered to come by and check later if she needed him to.

"Katie—"

She stopped him, holding up a hand. "You will tell me details of this post-concussive thing later—when I'm not feeling so murderous." She walked out the back door, letting the screen slam behind her.

Ford stretched out on the couch, intending to spend the rest of the day laying low. The faint whoosh of the ceiling fans in the quiet, dim house lulled him into a relaxed state as he let his mind drift, mulling over his daughter's anxiety and how he might help her.

CHAPTER NINETEEN

A FEW DAYS LATER, just as dusk turned the sky a soft blue, Katie leaned against the back door, soaking up the view of Ford sprawled in the grass, his t-shirt stretched taut across his shoulders, a hand propping up his head. Scarlett was rolling on and off his back while Miri lay in front of him looking up at the darkening sky, her expression earnest as she talked. She toyed with her daddy's other hand, obviously reveling in his focused attention. Katie watched for several moments, briefly wondering where Owen and the ever-frisky puppy were, before she remembered the puppy training classes Reggie had recruited Owen and Scout to join.

"MommyMommyMommy!" Scarlett spied her and ran to hug her legs tightly.

"Hey, Biscuit." Katie swooped the girl up for kisses.

"Hey, Mommy!" Miri called. Ford remained where he was but rolled over to look at her, his expression warm and open.

"Hey, Mommy." He reached out to tweak Miri's hair when she giggled at his echo. "Big sister, how about you and Scarlett get a bath going while I get Mommy her supper?"

To Katie's surprise, Miri readily agreed, pausing for a quick hug around her mother's waist as she took her little sister's hand, already talking about strawberry soap and tub toys.

"Supper?"

Close enough to hear her stomach rumble, Ford laughed. "You've always been one to miss meals when you're absorbed in a project. I assume emergency baking qualifies as a project, so I made sure to save you a plate. Let me bring it out here?" He gestured to the picnic table, leaning forward to buss her cheek with a light kiss on his way by. That kissing her cheek thing was becoming a habit, one she secretly enjoyed even as she persisted in keeping him at arm's length.

A few minutes later, Katie sat motionless, her eyes on the plate he'd set in front of her. Her hand shook just a little as she spread a napkin on her lap. The plate before her held a steak and vegetable kebab. The significance of the simple meal lay in the memory of the first meal Ford had made for her.

They had been together barely two months—two months in which they'd found time to spend together in the afternoons between morning and evening shifts. Afternoons when dappled sunlight bathed her bed where they lay, making love and talking about anything and everything except the future.

Katie had been shocked and terrified when she learned she was pregnant. Life experience in which her mother had died and her grief-stricken father committed suicide had led her to expect that nobody would choose to stay around in her life. Resolute, but with tears threatening, she told Ford about the pregnancy, insisting all she needed from him was money to ensure she could provide well enough for a baby. When Ford protested that he wasn't leaving her to handle things alone, she'd pragmatically reminded him that he was deploying in mere hours and his new life would begin—a life with no room for a girlfriend, much less a baby. Up until this moment, neither of them had spoken of the future beyond the few comments he'd made about keeping in touch through the mail and email—Katie didn't have Internet access at her run-down third floor walkup apartment, relying on the library. Ford had puzzled her with his reaction to her news—hugging her tightly and promising they'd talk more after he got them something to eat.

He'd left and gone down to the corner bodega to purchase a tiny steak (he knew she loved beef but could rarely afford it) and handful of vegetables that he turned into a supper of kebabs for two, which he served with glasses of milk, commenting that she needed to be sure to eat better from now on. They'd been seated on the couch with their plates on the wooden crate she used for a table when he'd dropped to a knee before her and asked her to marry him. The earnest twenty-two year old alone in the world thanks to his alcoholic father, bunking with a buddy while readying to deploy to a war zone for the first time, had convinced her that their baby deserved every effort they could make at a family. Ford had made her want to believe they could be different, that they could build a solid family like neither of them had.

And up until this past year, she'd thought they had done just that.

Coming back to the moment at hand, Katie looked across the table. His eyes were dark, almost navy blue with emotion, his expression tentative. Her eyes filled as she smiled slightly. "Thank you," she said softly.

Ford brushed his knuckles lightly across her cheek before moving away, leaving her to her thoughts.

While she ate, the sounds of the world around her lulled Katie into relaxing, bit by bit. She gave a few more minutes to thoughts of the days after Ford had deployed that first time. The oddity of suddenly being married, of being efficiently moved to base lodging by smiling young men who'd treated her as the cherished pregnant wife of their friend, of suddenly having a place in a world where up until then she'd existed alone at the fringes for so long. Suddenly she had friendly neighbors, a doctor, nurses, people she saw regularly who asked about her and looked out for her. As long as she lived, Katie would always think of those days as the beginning of her life.

Ten years later, here she was—at odds with the man who'd set all that into motion for her, with her. She sighed, sounds bringing her back to the present. The laughs and splashes of the girls playing in the bathtub wafted from the open windows, a dog or two barked, voices called back and forth as the shopkeepers on the street out front enjoyed families and tourists out for an evening stroll. Maybe it really was this easy, Katie thought, her eyes on Ford as he moved about the yard picking up kid toys, pausing to rest a hand on the big tree, looking up into the branches. Could they really mend and move forward? Katie sighed and forced herself to admit that mending couldn't truly happen if she continued to keep her secret—however inadvertently it had begun, it was now a problem.

CHAPTER TWENTY

"YOU NEED ME to stick around for the kids—or take them with me?" Ford stuck his head in the open bedroom door, Scarlett hanging from his back like a monkey.

Slipping her feet into red canvas shoes, Katie shook her head. "Reggie has a scavenger hunt ending with a pizza party going on with them. She'll bring them by the bar when they're done. We'll wrap girls' night up there. You just need to take Amos with you." The old man had spent the afternoon contentedly rocking on the patio out back where he'd watched Ford and Owen throw darts, regaling them with stories and tips. He was dozing on the front porch swing now, waiting for his supper at The Painted Parrot.

"So you'll meet me at the bar later?" Ford grinned, wiggling his eyebrows. "I'm totally going home with a hot girl—maybe even more than one," he sang out, swinging Scarlett around to kiss her nose and set her down.

"I'm a hot girl!" Scarlett nodded exuberantly.

"He meant Mom, silly," Owen scoffed at his littlest sister.

"And me, and Miri, O-wen," Scarlett sneered back.

Owen held up the four darts in his hand, careful to keep them pointed away from Scarlett. "One more round to be sure you're ready, Champ?"

Katie laughed. "Yeah, Champ, better polish that throw. These island guys are career dart junkies, you know."

Ford grabbed her around the waist and kissed her cheek as she headed for the door. Her pulse jumping at the touch of his lips, she leaned into him a little. His chest. Every time.

"Yeah, well, we Flying Aces are no slouches in the dart department. Hey, if I win, will you go out with me?"

Rolling her eyes, aware of their audience, she mock glared at him. "I'm married with children, Ford Callahan."

"Funny, Katie Callahan, so am I." He dropped his voice to a stage whisper and caught up with her in the hall, again snaking an arm around her waist. "If I win, will you let me walk you home along the beach?" His lips grazed the back of her neck, and she shivered, much to his delight.

"What has gotten into you? Stop touching me." She elbowed him hard then rolled her eyes for the benefit of the three kids looking on.

"I'm going over to the bakery to finish up the brownies. Miri, you and Scarlett take out the trash. Owen, the puppy fed and in his cage, same for the lizard. Pop over there when you're all ready to go."

Ford leaned against the kitchen counter, watching his wife command their circus with humor and sass, all three kids goofing off yet scattering to do her bidding.

Just as she reached the door, she turned back to look him up and down with a smoldering look that would have knocked his socks off if he'd been wearing any. "Maybe—if you win."

"Wait. Brownies?" he called after her retreating figure, once he had his breath back. Laughter was her reply.

All right then. Picking up the darts from the counter, he headed out back to practice one more time. Teasing or not, no way was he passing up the chance to win a walk alone with her. On the beach, in the dark.

Ford rubbed his chest thoughtfully, still staring after his wife. He was jolted from his thoughts by Owen's shout from out by where they'd hung the dartboard on a tree. "C'mon, Champ, one more go!"

Raising his arms high to the applause sounds his son was making, Ford jogged across the yard, tousling the boy's hair and taking the darts he offered.

CHAPTER TWENTY-ONE

"I SWEAR I COULD SMELL those brownies before I saw you, Katie. Mmmm." Charlie sniffed the air appreciatively.

"It's that very vivid imagination of yours, Charlie. No brownies here," Jill teased, waving one of the white bakery boxes under her friend's nose.

"I'm done walking. This is far enough from everyone," Katie announced, illustrating her point by kicking off her shoes and plopping down on the sand, taking care with the two boxes in her hands.

"Word, Sister." Jane spread out the flower-strewn beach blanket she carried, settling herself in one corner and reaching for Katie's boxes. "I'm done waiting to sample this stuff, too."

Katie laughed, setting the boxes on the blanket and reaching to unpack the mesh bag Jane had set down.

"Wine, check!" she called out.

"Brownies, check!" Charlie sang out.

"Sunset, check!" Jane joined in while Jill drew check marks in the air with a flourish.

"I call to order Girls' Night, where the only rule is that there must be much laughter. Wine and brownies optional, but strongly encouraged." Jill popped the cork and poured.

"Oh my stars, Katie, what is this?" Jane lifted a crusty brownie from the box, the caramel drizzle glittering with tiny salt crystals.

"My dears, behold the salted caramel pretzel-covered brownie— no catchy name for it yet. I just developed it yesterday. Taste, taste." Katie handed one to Charlie, Jill already helping herself.

"Oh my god, Katie, what have you done?" Charlie moaned, licking pretzel crumbs from her lips.

"I think you should call it Sweet 'n' Salty Chocolate Orgasm." Jill echoed Charlie's moan.

Katie laughed, "I'm sure Nash'll be impressed with that."

"And here I thought your little kavida tarts were my favorites—I must have more than one favorite, then." Jane closed her eyes and took another bite.

Katie nibbled on her own brownie, enjoying her friends' reaction to her latest experiment.

"I brought some of those, too. Just in case these, ya know, didn't hit the spot."

Jill nodded, "Right, just in case they weren't phenomenal like everything else that comes out of your kitchen."

The four sipped and nibbled, watching the show as the sun sank into the sea, the burst of colors drawing sighs and murmurs.

"New business first, I say." Charlie refilled her glass and handed the bottle off to Katie with a pointed look. "How's Ford after that episode?"

Katie waved a hand in the air. "You'd never know a thing was wrong unless you know what you're looking for. I've noticed he has headaches most days, but I had no idea they go that bad."

"But he can work?" Jill asked.

Nodding, Katie finished her brownie before replying, "Apparently so. He won't talk about it with me, but Gabe said he's fit."

"Okay, now you need to spill." Charlie pointed at Katie.

"What?" Katie, wide eyed, looked around the circle of expectant faces.

"What, she says." Jane nudged Katie's knee with her foot. "Spill."

"Seeing as you've been one of us for awhile now and the sheen of newness has worn to a comfortable patina, spill." Jill raised her glass in salute.

Charlie pushed back her hair and lay back on the blanket. "You've said a total of six words about 'the father of your children,' as you've called him, in the entire six months you've been here. Time to catch us up."

Katie laughed. "So he shows up and now I'm being forced to tell all?"

"Yep." Jill drew out the word dramatically, rolling over to rest her hands on her chin expectantly.

Katie sighed, stalling her friends by taking another sip of her wine. She considered another bite of her brownie, too, but figured that was pushing her luck and might get her dumped into the sea.

"Okay, the floor is open for questions—under extreme duress, I might add." She waved her glass in the air.

"Why didn't you tell us he's holy hotness?" Jane fanned herself dramatically.

"He is, isn't he?" Katie grinned. She'd just been admiring said holy hotness not an hour ago when a shirtless Ford had swung Miri down from the backyard tree.

"How long have you been married?" Jill started with an easy one.

"Ten years next month."

"Oooo, there's a story there." Jane's eyes widened.

Katie nodded, "Let's just say we both came from less than ideal backgrounds. Getting married was a huge step, as neither of us trusted easily." With a bone deep sigh, she gave up pretense. These were tried and true friends and she was tired of carrying it alone. "And I don't anymore."

"Ah, the real story surfaces. That's why you've not mentioned him much—trouble?" Charlie was serious now, reaching out to squeeze Katie's hand.

"I've—it's been easy to avoid it all since coming here. A fresh start in paradise, three kids and a bakery, so much to do."

"I just assumed you didn't want to talk about him while he was gone, kind of a denial that helps time pass." Jill patted her friend's leg.

"There's that, too," Katie agreed, opening the box of tarts in an effort to busy her hands. "Next question?" Letting them ask seemed easier than trying to find words for any of it.

"How long has he been in the military?" Jill nibbled on Katie's trademark treat.

"As long as I've known him." That one made Katie remember the smiling twenty-two-year-old boy determined to do something big.

"How many deployments?" Charlie topped off their glasses again, emptying the bottle into Katie's glass.

"Let's just say he's been deployed more than he's been home." Katie toyed with a thread on the blanket, wrapping it around her finger and off again.

"Oh, wow. So that means serious adjustment with him being home for good, huh? I remember well how hard it was when my dad came home—for all of us," Jane said.

"Obviously it's more than that, after your trust comment earlier," Charlie prodded.

"Until he came in the door here, we hadn't spoken one on one in almost eight months," Katie said quietly. "By choice."

Jill whistled.

"What happened? Something besides war, I'd guess, because I bet you rock the military wife thing." Jill felt as if she'd neglected to really tune in to her friend in the past few months. Then again, it took time to build trust, and it had been a year full of challenges and changes for the island.

Katie took a deep breath, filling her lungs with the salty air, looking out to the sea. The midnight blue water ebbed and flowed as it had for centuries and would for centuries more, its soothing sound now permanent background music in her daily life. "I—um. Well." She blew out a breath. "One part of the long story is that he got hurt—nearly died—and wouldn't come home until he was well. It's been six months of healing alone—he wouldn't let me help him."

Jill's eyes filled with tears. "That's hard."

Charlie reached over to hold Katie's hand. "You had to feel abandoned."

Katie nodded. "It's so hard to understand why he'd spend six months in pain, refusing my help—he wouldn't even talk to me for almost two months of that. When he did call, I shut him out, leaving him to talk to the kids."

"Whoa." This from Jane with an echo from Charlie.

"Now what?" This from Jill.

"Once I came here and found Amos, I packed up the kids and moved. I sent an email telling Ford where to find us. When he showed up, I tried to get him a room at the B&B, but he wouldn't have it. We're dealing moment by moment." Katie gave a relieved sigh. "It's actually good to share about it now. It was like if I didn't talk about it, he would be okay—we would be okay. Now that he's here, I don't know."

Her friends nodded sympathetically, all scooting closer in support.

"Him being here, safe and sound, is a start," Charlie said.

"It is, and it should be all that matters, but there's so much anger." Katie looked around at her friends. "I'm glad I have the three of you."

"There's nothing so priceless as girlfriends." Jane raised her mostly empty glass to the others, who joined her in the toast with their last swallows.

"So you and Ford haven't talked about it yet?" Charlie posed the question carefully, wanting to avoid sounding accusatory.

"We've yelled a couple times, but no. It's mostly been avoidance—I know, I know." Katie made a face.

"While I do believe you've got to sit down and really talk it out, I also know that sometimes you just have to get through the days. The fact that he's here and you're working on it has got to matter—a lot." Charlie smiled reassuringly.

Katie smiled back, "Exactly. Okay enough about me for now, moving on."

"Before we join the rowdy crew down there, I have a mom question." Jill waved a hand in the direction of The Painted Parrot, its lights faintly visible down the beach.

"I love mom questions," Katie said, relieved they accepted the shift in conversation easily.

"Okay, well, um. What if you're making love with your husband with noisy, glorious abandon—"

Charlie hooted out loud, "Noisy, glorious abandon, she says."

Jill rolled her eyes. "Well, it was...yeah, so..." She felt her cheeks heat a little, but she pressed on with a glare to a chuckling Charlie, "As I was saying, if you're doing so and when it's all over, you're still clinging to him, catching your breath...then realize the baby, who *was* sleeping in his bed in the corner, is—"

Katie started laughing, nearly falling over with glee.

"Wait, wait for it!" Jill held out her hands in a wide sweeping gesture, speaking the next words with slow emphasis, "You realize the baby is awake—and standing up in his crib, wide eyed and terrified."

All three of her friends gave up trying to hold it together and fell over on the blanket amid peals of laughter.

Jane was the first to recover somewhat. "I'm not a mom, but he's too little to remember, anyway, right?" She snickered on the last few words.

"Well, yeah, but he was terrified! Witnessing that—um, no covers were in sight, by the way—won't damage him? Give him some vague, unexplained fears or nightmares?" Jill was seriously worried, yet another giggle slipped through in spite of it.

Charlie gasped for air and shoved herself upright, reaching out to squeeze Jill in a hug.

Katie did the same, desperately trying to stop laughing.

"Honey, most likely he was just confused as opposed to terrified," Charlie said.

Katie nodded her agreement, still not trusting her voice.

"Whew," Jane breathed, joining the group hug. "Let's go find some good-looking men to buy us drinks."

"Speaking of, you gonna put intentional moves on our sheriff?" Jill elbowed Jane as they all stood, gathering up things and finding shoes in the sand.

"Girl, don't flirt with him, just flat out come on to the guy," Charlie advised.

Jane nodded, folding her end of the blanket into the two ends Katie held up. "That's the plan. I'm done being subtle."

"Whoot, he has no chance!" Katie teased as they began the walk down the beach to The Painted Parrot, the edge of the waves lapping at their feet.

Katie realized she felt relaxed and happy for the first time in eons. It was nice, the absence of that icy ball of fear that had lived inside her the entire time Ford had been gone. He was here, he was safe. They'd drink and laugh with their friends, go home and tuck their children into bed. This was more than enough. It had to be.

CHAPTER TWENTY-TWO

THE PAINTED PARROT was brightly lit in the waning daylight, the lights inside spilling out onto the sand along with music and laughter. Ford took his time walking down the beach, taking part in the island's daily appreciation of the view as the sun set into the sea with a blaze of glory. It turned out that the myth he'd heard about the sky turning blue at sunset was no myth out here. Every night just as the sun set, a faint indigo flash turned day into night, just like that. He had to admit that, while they were a long way from familiar territory, the island was an incredible place to live. Visiting was a shiny gift, living here was striking gold.

As Ford stepped inside the bar for his first Painted Parrot evening, Gabe spotted him and called out, waving the bottle he was using to mix a drink, "Hey, Ford, c'mon in!"

Ford waved a greeting and made his way across the filled bar to an empty seat next to Amos. He'd used Nash's golf cart to drop Amos at the edge of the small parking lot where a shell path led to the bar. Because he planned to walk home with his family, he'd returned the cart to the shed and enjoyed the sunset walk back.

"Your big-mouthed boy says you're gonna kick our collective asses at the dart board." Nash, next to Gabe behind the bar, pointed a finger at Ford with an affected snarl.

"My kid does have a big mouth, but he ain't no liar," Ford volleyed back.

Gabe hooted out loud, high-fiving him with one hand, the other setting a beer in front of him.

Neatly intercepting the bar towel Nash threw at his head, Ford sent it back without missing a beat.

"So what's for supper, Papa?" He turned to Amos.

"Oh, we're eating? I am rather hungry." Amos smiled, his fingers shredding the napkin his drink had been sitting on.

Gabe glanced at Amos, then at Ford, a frown furrowing his brow. Ford caught the glance and gave a slight shrug.

"Yep, Papa, it's suppertime." Ford patted the old man's shoulder.

Gabe came down to lean on the bar in front of Amos. "Jill's bringing us some of that gumbo, how's that sound?"

"I'm not sure I've had it before, but I'm sure game to try something new." Amos nodded his head, shredding the napkin into even smaller pieces.

Nash's face lit up as Jill came around the corner, plates already in hand. Amos always ate whatever she brought him, without fail. "Hey, pretty lady!"

"Back at ya, hot stuff!" Jill winked at him as she settled the plates in front of Amos.

"One of your favorites, Papa." She kissed his cheek, sweeping away the shredded napkin and replacing it with a fresh one. "I'm off!" She kissed her fingers, wiggled them at Nash and grabbed a couple of wine bottles from the glass-front cooler behind the bar. "Only the good stuff for us girls." Waving to Ford and Amos, she left the bar and headed down the beach, her short yellow skirt blowing in the breeze.

Nash watched her go.

"Close your mouth 'fore you catch flies, fella," Amos cackled, the laugh turning into a mild coughing fit. Ford slid the old man's water glass closer and thumped him on the back.

"There we go," he said when the cough had settled and Amos resumed eating.

Ford sat back in his seat, half turned from the bar to the view outside, with the room behind him.

As the idyllic island evening settled in, the periwinkle-streaked sky faded into the deep sapphire blue sea. The stars winked along the horizon, and a few boat and buoy lights danced on the sea. Ford breathed deeply.

The Painted Parrot's evening in full swing, Gabe was mingling about the room with his customers. He laughed easily, shared secret hideaway locations with newlyweds and second honeymooners alike, held up his hands in exaggerated fishing measurements and added visitors to his charter list for the next day. Nash kept the drinks and jokes flowing, his boisterous laughter contagious. Luke and Tag came in, and the darts tournament began in earnest, every man for himself. The competition was fierce, with regulars and tourists alike stepping up to the line.

During the last two rounds of the tournament, Jill returned along with Katie, Charlie and Jane. When they walked in, Nash was at the line.

"Nashman!" Jill whooped, bringing a big grin to her husband's face as he gave her a salute and set up his shot. Scoring perfectly, Nash strutted over to his wife amid the catcalls and cheers, kissing her soundly to the enjoyment of the crowd. When he pulled away, tugging her along behind him to return to the bar, Jill fanned herself dramatically. "I'm taking this one home with me!"

"Do I get a kiss like that?" Gabe called to Charlie, taking up his place at the line.

"Score like that and sure!" Charlie laughed, pushing back her hair as she made her way across the room, talking to customers along the way. These days, she was just as much a part of The Painted Parrot's allure as her husband.

The women stood around the bar, laughing while Luke described Ford's dismal opening throw. Jane patted Ford's shoulder while elbowing Luke. "You're just jealous, Sheriff!"

Ford shrugged and raised his bottle. Since he'd more than redeemed himself in the following turns, he could let the embarrassing moment go—especially since neither Katie nor Owen had been there to witness it. With most of the seats along the deep bar full, Ford stood, motioning for Katie to take his seat. With a smile, she slid onto the rattan seat, looking around.

"Bill took Amos home a while ago, he was falling asleep in his corner." Ford's breath blew against her ear, ostensibly to be heard above the noise as the bar erupted in response to Gabe narrowly pulling ahead of Nash in points.

She shivered slightly, as he'd expected. "Thanks. I meant to call and check on him, but got sidetracked."

"I'd like to think that was because you knew he was in good hands."

Her expression going blank, she replied, "You'd think." She just couldn't bring herself to depend on him, choosing to largely act as if he were just passing through.

"When will the kids be here?" He looked around the room, seeing a kid or two run past.

"Any minute now. Reggie texted that they were on their way."

Sure enough, just as Ford moved away to take his last turn at the dartboard, Reggie and her entourage came through door. "Holler if your kid doesn't find you!" she bellowed over the din, the kids scattering throughout the place. She stayed by the door until she saw all the kids find where they belonged.

Owen and his sisters found Katie's side in short order, Amos's customary seat a common meeting point for them.

Katie listened to her girls and Rory chatter about the evening, while Owen climbed to sit atop the end of the bar in order to see his father's moves.

Reggie found her way up to the bar, setting Zane next to Owen. Behind the bar, Jill took the baby from her, kissing his fuzzy head as he nuzzled her neck. The room erupted in cheers that startled the baby wide eyed, but he didn't cry. He'd been around this enough to know all was well as long as familiar arms held him.

Ford's last throws were flawless, and he shamelessly bowed to the noisy crowd before holding up both hands in a victory salute.

"There should be a prize for that kind of throwing!" Jane called out.

"There is—I get to walk a pretty lady home!" Ford answered, bowing in Katie's direction with a grin.

Katie laughed, prompting the little girls leaning on her to blow him a kiss. Owen was already beaming at Ford's side, having been the first to high-five his dad. The boy stood with Ford's arm slung around his shoulders, looking like it was the happiest night of his life. Katie felt her heart tug at the sight and pulled her cell phone out to snap a picture.

Charlie leaned over the trio of small people to nudge her friend. "Let me take the kids home with us tonight." When Katie started to protest, Charlie insisted, "It's time you two had some time alone."

Katie tried to object again, "We're far from...well, from that point."

"That point or not, you can talk at ease for a change. Or not talk at all."

Charlie's eyebrow wiggle made Katie laugh. "Okay, okay."

"C'mon kids, let's get out of here. Owen, if you come along, Gabe will take you with him fishing at oh-dark-thirty in the morning." Charlie knew the nearly ten-year-old boy would hesitate at being lumped in with a trio of little girls, but he loved going fishing with Gabe.

Sure enough, she was rewarded with a grin as Owen looked up at Ford. "You want to go fishing, too, Dad?"

"Maybe we'll have better luck than we did this morning," Gabe chimed in from where he leaned on the bar, baby Zane encircled in his arms, valiantly trying to crawl further down the bar.

Ford glanced at Katie before replying, "We'll see."

Katie blushed as their friends teased them both.

Gabe handed the reaching baby over to Nash and took over the drinks the other man had just mixed. Nash pointed out the customers to whom the drinks belonged, and Gabe rounded the bar to serve them.

Ford leaned down in response to Miri's tug on his arm.

"You'll be home with Mommy when we get back?" Her big blue eyes were worried under her crinkled brow.

"I'm not going anywhere off this island, Miribelle." He kissed her cheek, then her sister's.

Little arms hugged his neck tightly, tiny lips kissed both his cheeks.

"Wait up for me, my love," Gabe called as Charlie made her way across the bar, surrounded by jumping, chattering kids, followed closely by Jill with Zane in her arms. Charlie waved a hand airily without turning around.

Ford looked down at Katie, a slight smile on his face at her wide eyes. She was nervous. Hell, if he was honest, he'd admit to being nervous, too. He had no idea what to expect. For all he knew, she'd ditch him and lock herself in the bakery for the night. He hoped not, but who knew?

Holding out his hand to her, the cacophony around them faded and the world seemed to narrow to just the two of them.

She took his hand and hopped down from the barstool. Barely noticing Jane's goodbye and Nash's teasing remarks, she walked close to his side as they left The Painted Parrot and went out into the night.

CHAPTER TWENTY-THREE

HER HAND LOOSE in his, Ford led them down to walk along the water's edge.

Pausing a step ahead of him, she turned to put her hands on his shoulders for balance and toed off her shoes. Before she could bend to pick them up, Ford put his hands on her waist and leaned in for a kiss. "I thought I'd set the tone for the night," he said against her lips, keeping the kiss light and undemanding.

"Mmm, nice tone," she murmured, tiptoeing to deepen the kiss. It had been so long since she'd really kissed him. Since he'd really kissed her.

Bathed in the light of the moon, kissing her with the sea swirling at their feet, Ford slid his hands up her sides slowly, cupping her face just so and slipped his tongue inside without hesitation. His moan was instant and deep, matching hers.

Fireworks exploded behind Katie's closed eyelids as their tongues celebrated a long awaited reunion, their bodies pressing together as if they needed the contact to live.

They both jumped apart when a stern voice said, "Get a room, will you? You're about to commit public indecency—or something." Luke burst out laughing at their twin expressions of guilt.

With a growl, Ford shot a foot out to trip the sheriff, but Luke was too quick, dancing back a step.

Hanging onto Luke's arm, Jane laughed as they passed by, shooting Katie a meaningful look over her shoulder. Katie pointed at Luke's back and made a grabbing motion to her friend. It appeared that Jane might take with both hands the girls' night advice she'd been given. Tonight might just be a truly incredible night for love here on the island.

Katie dropped her head to Ford's chest, the giggles Luke had spurred threatening to consume her.

Said giggles must have been catching, as she could feel the rumble of Ford's chuckle in his chest. She sighed against him, her hands sliding around his waist to fist in the back of his shirt and pull him closer.

The chuckles and giggles faded as Ford wrapped his arms around her. He felt something deep down inside him loosen and slowly spool free. Something he hadn't even realized had been tight since the last time he'd deployed. She was home for him, and as long as they were apart, he'd be searching, seeking, never truly at rest.

Ford rested his chin atop her head, gazing out into the night. The moon was bright, its dancing reflection as hypnotic and enchanting as the music of the waves. While he would have never dreamed they'd be here at the edge of the world, Ford found himself believing in the magic of paradise, hoping in the magic of paradise.

His lips met hers again. He couldn't get enough. Holding her face in his hands, Ford pulled back from the kiss, teasing her by tracing her lips with the tip of his tongue. All the way down her bottom lip, spending extra time nibbling at the corner, slipping inside only to dart back out and tantalizingly trace her top lip the same way. The breathy sighs she made were twisting him all up in knots inside. He found he wanted her to make those sighs again. He wanted to hear his name in that breathless way.

Both breathing a little fast, they walked up the beach, the lights of the town beckoning them. Katie laughed as Ford increased their pace across the park, almost towing her along behind him. She tugged his arm to stop him before they passed the swings, dimly lit by the lights of the town around it.

Ford went to the swings and held one for her gallantly. Once she was settled, he stood in front of it and pulled her close, swing and all. His hands over hers on the swing chains, he bent to whisper, "Remember the park near your building way back when?"

"Why do you think I wanted to swing for a minute?"

He let the swing go, once, then twice, catching her when it swung back to him the third time.

This time when he bent to kiss her, she buried her head in his neck and held him close, wrapping her arms and legs around him to keep the swing motionless.

"Ah, Katie, you're killing me," he ground out as she nipped his neck, soothing the stings with flicks of her tongue. He lifted her from the swing to stand on the ground. She kissed her way across his collarbone with agonizing slowness. "Mmm," she murmured, "Let's get home—and hurry."

Ford rolled his eyes, pretty sure that *she* was the one who'd stopped at the damn swings.

They hurried across the rest of the park, slowing only once they'd crossed the street to the porch of the little blue house. Once there, Ford reached inside the door to flip off the porch light, leaving only the string of fairy lights lit. He sat in the porch hammock, positioning Katie between his legs, giving him easy access to her. Yeah, it had been far, far too long. As he kissed his way down her neck, her arms came around him, her hands caressing his nape, fingers tangling in his hair. She hiked up her skirt and, Lord help him, straddled his lap, sending the hammock swaying lightly.

"I have died and gone to heaven—or hell, depending on which one has bewitching angels."

Katie laughed softly as she kissed him, holding him close. She leaned back a little, took his hands and brought them to her breasts, her eyes deep pools in the moonlight.

His hands trembled as he caressed her through the shirt then moved to unbutton and push it aside reverently. He'd dreamed of this so many times—and feared he'd lost it forever just as many times.

"Always have, always will," he whispered the words he'd used time and again, his hands touching her ever so gently, his mouth taking hers again.

The air was heavy with hibiscus, the scent on the sea breeze adding to the intoxication of the moment. Breathing grew heavy and faster, soft gasps and sighs were punctuated with groans and muttered curses as limits were reached, stretched.

At some point, when his mind was a complete blur and he thought he'd explode, Katie climbed off Ford's lap, took his hand and led him in to the cottage.

"I can't promise this changes anything." Her voice was husky and low. "But this is one thing we know works well, Ace." She smiled at him in the near darkness, tugging him along the hallway to the bedroom.

Ford swallowed hard. "I couldn't have said it better myself."

With the moon as their only light, the sea waves coupled with sighs and murmurs as their music, Ford and Katie reminded each other of all they had shared together, all they had missed and all they had yet to give.

CHAPTER TWENTY-FOUR

KATIE WOKE WITH A START, unaccustomed to sleeping for long without checking on the kids or waking with Ford on her mind when he was across the world. She breathed deeply and snuggled in with a sigh when she remembered the kids were with Charlie, and Ford...well, he was certainly on her mind as he was what she'd just snuggled into, warm and solid, wrapped around her. As she started to drift back off, she felt his muscles tense slightly, then relax as he woke fully.

"Do you always wake up at the ready?" Her fingers danced across his arm where it lay across her chest.

Tightening said arm, he brought his body into full contact with hers. His sleep-roughened voice rumbling in her ear, he pressed himself snugly against her. "This kind of ready? That's always been you."

Wordlessly, she turned to trace his face with her fingertips, looping a leg over his and scooting into him. She'd acted on instinct and memory last night, who was to say that couldn't continue before dawn crept up the sky?

* * *

The travel mug of coffee on the nightstand with a sticky note attached did a little to ease the heavy feeling that had settled somewhere in his chest when Ford woke to an empty bed. He couldn't help his automatic dread of what Katie would say—or not say—in the light of day. While he knew one night of lovemaking didn't fix everything, he could hope, couldn't he? Rolling to his side, he read the sticky note through bleary morning eyes and grinned. *Time to make the doughnuts.* That laugh helped.

Sipping the coffee, he moved to shower amid the lingering steam of Katie's lavender scent and got a move on out the door. He didn't want Nash and Gabe to have to wait on him. The air was balmy and fresh to his sand-scarred lungs. He wondered anew if he'd ever take sand-free for granted again. The town stirred to life, a light flickering on here and there, as those who made a living fishing or from the fish brought in—and those who made the doughnuts—started their day before the sun rose The ever-present breeze riffled the tree leaves, the chirping fruit bats settling in while the parrots and lorikeets ramped up to greet the day. Ford paused on the porch, looking over at the bakery's brightly lit back windows. He saw Katie pass by the window, laughing, carrying a tray up high, as if she were stepping over or around something. This was a moment of rare peace, one where he felt that just maybe a bridge—albeit a shaky one—had been built between himself and his wife.

*   *   *

The day passed in a blur of activity for Katie, with kids to juggle, pies to be baked, store to be minded, projects to be worked on—and a here-in-the-flesh husband to consider. Her world spun rather smoothly as long as she didn't dwell on what might be—or might not be—when it came to Ford. Even if they did find their way back, could their marriage survive her accidental secret? With a shake of her head, Katie pushed her thoughts aside and focused on the task in front of her.

When Ford and Owen had stopped by the bakery after fishing, Katie had genuinely been happy to see him, saved from much reaction by the fact that her hands were buried in a huge bowl of dough. She might not know just where they stood, what the future held, but she didn't allow herself regrets over the night before. They'd both needed that desperately. She'd pointed Ford and Owen to a corner table where a plate of muffins waited, Owen eating enough for the both of them in one sitting. The two had then disappeared to help Nash with something or other.

Laughing off a text from Jill demanding to know how the night before had gone, Katie teased her friend with a flippant reply, *Sleep is king.*

As the afternoon waned on, a frantic customer called the bakery phone to beg Katie for a last minute birthday cake and cookie order—last minute as in by tomorrow afternoon. With Reggie off for the evening, Katie automatically started to refuse, to explain that she had kids to juggle too, when she stopped. If they had any hope of moving forward, she had to make some efforts too. Chewing her lip for a moment, she took her phone from the dock on the counter and texted Ford, asking if he'd round up the kids and handle supper.

His reply text made her smile: *Sure thing. But don't work too hard, Katiebean.*

With that, she returned to the customer she'd put on hold and made her day with a promise that she could have something ready. Such moments were excellent word-of-mouth fodder for the newish baker on the island. Bakery closed, music cranked and clock ticking, Katie got into her zone with a grin. It was nice to have parental backup again, despite the cost leaning on him might be to her in the long run.

*   *   *

It pleased Ford to no end that Katie was finally treating him like a partner instead of a half-invalid visitor. That fact, coupled with the warmth of yesterday still curling low inside him, put a fresh spring in his step as he and the older kids picked up Scarlett from Jill's and swung by the grocery on their way home.

While the constant chaos and chatter of life with three kids was taking him some time to get used to—they were so unpredictable and loud, and he couldn't just order them to clean up or shut up like he could a bunch of unruly soldiers—Ford no longer felt like a giant bundle of exposed, jangling nerves. Most of the time, anyway. Rather than shoo the kids off to play, Ford put all three of them to work in the kitchen with him. Immersion or trial by fire, take your pick. He tapped into the contentment that still ran through him, telling himself that the ticking time bomb feeling was just part of dealing with his residual head stuff and part of reentry into daily life.

CHAPTER TWENTY-FIVE

BRIGHTLY COLORED BANNERS waved in the island breeze as every stall in the park was decked out even more than usual to draw the eye of passersby. In addition to the usual open market stalls that were always in the park, temporary booths were scattered about as the celebration was in full swing. Music and laughter filled the air, keeping a smile on Katie's face as she refilled the sampler trays with bite-sized versions of her popular hand pies, slapping away a hand that came from behind her. "You've had more than your fill, Ace."

Ford laughed, squeezing her around the waist with one arm, the other arm full of a chattering little girl. "Mommy! Mommy, Daddy said I can go on the boat today!" Scarlett's eyes were wide, her mouth a perfect O of excitement. Katie turned, leaning into Ford and kissing the girl's warm, slightly sticky cheek. "Cotton candy already, huh?"

Scarlett clapped her hands. "PINK cotton candy!"

"A little sampler cone." Ford winked at his wife. She noticed the slight squint to his eyes was a little more pronounced than it had been earlier and brought a hand up to smooth the creases.

"I'm fine." He shrugged off her concern, his smile softening the action. "I'm on call, and you know a day like today will be crazy."

"No doubt. Just let me know and I'll meet you to take Scarlett."

"I'll likely swing back by here on my way to wherever."

"Daddy! Daddy, boat time!" Scarlett kicked her legs to get down.

"Go. Boat." Katie laughed at Ford's quick reflexes in swinging the girl with the whirling feet down without mishap. He wiped his brow in an affected motion of relief, his quick sideways grin and wink rewarded by her slight blush and shove. "Go. Boat," she repeated.

With another wink at Katie, Ford looked down at his dancing daughter. "Let's boat, Biscuit." He held out a hand to her, the other one briefly rubbing his forehead.

Katie watched him stride away, Scarlett skipping by his side. He'd been gone most of the day today, making runs early with Luke and the squad. She admitted to holding her breath when he'd first started, unsure if being back to work as a medic would trigger any adverse reactions for him. She frequently reminded herself sternly that all returning soldiers didn't suffer from PTSD. She'd been watching Ford with an eagle eye, but his restlessness seemed to be directly related to the residual pain he lived with and his quest to find a groove in the new world order he was now a part of.

"Mountain berry tarts are going fast like always, Bosslady!" Reggie's cheerful voice pulled Katie from her thoughts.

Both the trays of free tiny tarts and hand pies for purchase were nearly empty again.

"They're a crowd pleaser, aren't they? Let's add the cookies and the petit fours to the mix, shall we?"

"Ooo, I love your petit fours. I'll take a half dozen!" Jill stopped in front of the booth, Zane cheerfully kicking from her hip where he rode in a brightly colored handmade sling. Katie handed the baby a cookie while Reggie boxed up the treats.

"Ahem." Jill eyed Katie meaningfully.

"Hmmm?" Katie raised her eyebrows, busying herself with refilling the sample trays.

"Um, I've not gotten a single text about your big night alone with your hot Flying Ace, missy. Lots of texts about this or about that, every single one a disappointment." Jill fake nibbled the soggy cookie Zane shoved at her mouth. "Mmm, good cookie! I'll eat it all!"

The baby chortled, snatching his cookie back. Predictably, the two women laughed at him, causing Zane to ham it up even more. "Such a shy child, this one."

"Disappointing texts suck." Katie moved to help a customer or two, meeting her friend's glare with a grin. Jill wiped the baby clean, strapped a toy to his wrist, and waited, foot tapping impatiently.

"Something, anything, Katie!"

As the customers walked away, Katie grinned. "We still got it."
She immediately slapped a hand over her mouth. "I did not mean to
say that out loud."

Jill whooped, fist pumping the air.

Katie sobered. "But it doesn't change anything."

"What a crock. Pasta at your house later?" Jill grabbed her son's
hands, saving a passing child's hair from a painful tug.

"You know it." Katie blew baby Zane a kiss, which he gleefully
returned with a noisy smack as Jill left to check on her soap booth
where she'd left Rory and Miri in charge.

Watching her friend go, Katie laughed to herself, remembering
the story of how the last time Jill left that duo in charge of her booth,
the girls had cheerfully given away 'the bigger samples' after the
basket of samples was empty. Today, Gabe was supervising from
The Painted Parrot booth next to them, making sure the merchandise
didn't become 'bigger samples' this year.

CHAPTER TWENTY-SIX

BREATHING HARD, his heart pounding out of his chest and his vision blurred, Ford sat motionless on the beach. One minute he'd been running along the shore, the next minute the world had spun upside down, leaving him groping for something to grab onto as he'd crashed to the sand.

"Where the hell did that come from?" he growled, head in his hands, eyes closed tightly. Despite his frustration and anger at being knocked helpless, Ford had to admit he'd ignored the warning signs all day. Post-concussive recuperation, for him, had involved learning his body's signals that he needed to rest. By rest, it meant he had to come to a full stop, down flat and silent for the duration. If he didn't, his stubborn body forced his hand no matter where he was or what he was doing.

While he lay there, his desperate need to be whole and healthy for his family took over his mind. They didn't need this stress of worrying about him falling over midstride in front of them or getting hurt doing so. In light of Miri's fears, witnessing such would be devastating for her. The more he thought about it, a solution began to form. It wasn't a good solution, but it was a workable, best of a bad situation, solution.

Knowing it could be hours before the world settled enough for him to stand, much less walk the miles back to town, Ford fumbled with his phone. He sent a text and lay back on the sand to wait, arm over his eyes.

CHAPTER TWENTY-SEVEN

IN KATIE'S KITCHEN, Charlie sat atop the counter, Jill perched on a barstool next to her. "What do you mean it can't last?" The air redolent with spices and tomato sauce, Charlie spoke as she grated Parmesan cheese for one of her trademark pasta dishes. The expats, while supremely happy and acclimated to island life, gathered together to cook and eat familiar favorites now and again. Some things just couldn't be replicated in The Painted Parrot's kitchen—even by Matteo. As good friends do, Charlie and Jill were grilling Katie on her night alone with Ford.

Katie put a lid on the pasta sauce and turned from the stove. Glancing around to ensure the kids were still out back, she kept her voice low. "Two reasons. One, I can't get past the fact that Ford chose struggling alone over coming home to me after nearly being killed. Two...oh, never mind—one is enough."

"Oh, no, this time you don't." Jill waved a fork in the air. As a nursing mother, she'd been dished up a plate as soon as the food was ready. With Zane sleeping soundly on the living room floor, time was of the essence.

"Katie, honey, you have brought it up several times only to back off. Maybe sharing with us will help somehow?" Charlie asked gently, the distress evident on Katie's face. She was beginning to really worry for her friend; the last few times they'd crossed paths, Katie had seemed unusually distracted.

Leaning on the counter between her friends, Katie dropped her face into her hands. "Mother of God, I still can't believe he's here, safe and whole." She let a breath out slowly.

Jill one-arm hugged her friend, meeting Charlie's eyes over Katie's head.

Before either of them could speak, Katie continued, "But at the same time, seeing him all the time now is like a knife twisting in my heart, knowing we can't fix this. Knowing it can't last."

Charlie covered the bowl of grated cheese, moving everything off to the side. She stroked Katie's shoulder, rubbing the tense muscles there. "Honey, you're going to have to talk about this with him. You know how half the time we misunderstand what the guys are thinking without talking it out."

Katie nodded, her face still in her hands. She took a deep, shuddery breath and looked at Jill, then Charlie, her eyes filling with tears. "I saw pictures from the incident for the first time the other day."

Jill's eyes widened, and Charlie raised an eyebrow.

In the blink of an eye, the room was filled with the shouts of kids and the laughter of men. The baby was scooped up by his father, some kids reached for the sink to wash up, others ran down the hall to the bathroom sink.

Katie turned away, buying herself a moment in pretending the sauce needed a stir. Charlie laughed at something Gabe said as she hopped down from the counter and reached into the cabinet for bowls. Her voice low, for Katie's ears only, she said, "Let's beach walk in a bit."

Katie nodded, her expression pensive. Game face, she told herself as she dropped a ladle into the sauce pot and set it on the counter next to the pasta. Scarlett hugged her mother's legs, her grin bringing a smile to Katie's face as she dampened a paper towel to wash the island dirt off the little girl's face. Busying herself with helping the kids fill their bowls and cups, she avoided making eye contact with anyone, especially Ford—fully aware that she'd never done a game face very well.

* * *

In the master bathroom, Ford splashed water on his face and stood, arms braced on the vanity. His chest was tight, his mouth dry, but this time it wasn't a migraine or a panic attack. He'd walked up to the back door just before the rest of the crew, just in time to hear

Katie say that seeing him hurt her, that she didn't believe they could fix this. The sorrow in her voice, the defeated slump to her body had nearly brought him to his knees. Up until yesterday's episode on the beach had turned him inside out, he'd believed that being present, shoring up this life they shared one moment at a time, would eventually work for them. He wasn't so stupid as to think that making love the other night had solved anything, but he had thought it was a step in the right direction. After seeing her in the kitchen just now, he wasn't so sure.

*   *   *

With kids and men heartily playing pirates and more pirates, Charlie rose from her chair at the table outside. She met Jill's eyes and tipped her head towards the door where Katie had gone inside a few minutes ago. Jill dropped a light blanket over Zane, asleep in his playpen.

"Beach walking," Charlie called, and Gabe waved an arm in response, his back covered by two kids brandishing foam pirate swords. Ford, opposite Gabe, was buried under more kids swinging swords while Nash sat smugly in the tree, looking down on it all. "All hail the Pirate King!"

"As if," Ford bellowed, a quick tug bringing Nash crashing to the ground where he expertly tucked and rolled.

Jill and Charlie found Katie at the sink, absently washing a dish while she gazed out the window. "Come on." Charlie took Katie's arm and pulled her away, Jill handing her a towel.

Katie dried her hands and let them lead her out the door. The trio walked across the park holding hands without talking, stopping at the sand's edge to kick off shoes. They walked down to the water's edge and sat just out of the tide's reach, Katie between Jill and Charlie.

"You saw some pictures?" Charlie didn't waste time getting right to it. With five kids and three husbands—all three on call for various things—time to talk could be cut off at any moment.

Katie sat cross legged, drawing aimless circles in the sand. "Ford hasn't been active duty for over eight months."

Jill frowned, "But that's about the time you moved here—without him."

Katie nodded, drawing in a deep breath and letting it out slowly. "He got hurt—nearly blown to pieces—about a month before I came here."

"Oh, honey," Charlie murmured.

"Bad, then?" Jill asked.

"It's bad when they call to tell you he hasn't died yet. Five nights in a row they called, every call they told me he'd likely not make it through the night." Katie brushed tears from her cheeks.

"Why couldn't you get to him by then? I thought there was a system for such situations." Jill frowned.

"There is. They came for me. I—I was—" Katie paused on a sob, pressing her fist to her mouth. The secret was so heavy she could hardly breathe. Did she dare tell her friends, did she dare hope they'd not abandon her when they learned what she'd done? No, if it were ever shared, Ford deserved to know first.

Drawing on the strength that had always served her well since she was ten years old, Katie wiped away her tears and pushed to her feet to pace, she needed to get a solid grip on herself. She could tell them enough without sharing her secret. Then maybe it would be okay. "I-I couldn't go immediately. By the time I got there, he was awake and had decided it would too much of a burden for me to take care of him in his condition. He decided it would be better if he handled his recovery alone. He wouldn't even let me in to see him. While I was still his next of kin and still consulted in general, they couldn't go against his wishes on letting me in to see him—not without upsetting him. Until he showed up in my living room here, I hadn't laid eyes on him since two months after the incident—and then it was only via Skype."

"Oh, dear God," Jill breathed.

"No wonder you're angry," Charlie said.

Splashing at the edge of the sea, Katie turned back to her friends. "Well, before you share my righteous anger, you should know that I did not react well. I shut him out in return. That Skype call? It was the only time I spoke to him until he showed up here. The kids answered his calls, I emailed him a homefront status report once a month or so. If he didn't need me, then I didn't need him." She crossed her arms defensively. "He showed up here just like that, and I've been reeling since. It's both relief and pain every time I hear his voice, look at him."

Charlie stood, going to Katie and wrapping her arms around her.

"I'm so sorry, honey. I wish we had known, we've not really been there for you all this time."

Jill joined them and the three simply hugged for several minutes.

"Yes, you have. You've accepted me and you've helped me build a circle of people I can depend on."

"We are that." Charlie patted Katie's back.

"It seems like you're making progress, though," Jill said. "I mean, he's here, living with you and you shared a great night, right?"

Katie smiled slightly. "I felt whole again, I always did with him."

"But?" Charlie prompted.

"He was broken in those pictures I saw." She whispered, the pictures flashing through her mind. "Broken so that it took weeks for him to even be fully lucid and able to sit upright. He nearly died more than once and spent months trying to get back on his feet, yet he didn't let me come to him, he didn't come home when he could have. He shut me out. In the middle of all that, I needed him more than I've ever needed him and because of the mess, I couldn't tell him so. I don't know how to trust him anymore." Anger returned to replace the tears.

"Maybe you both have to remember what you had before and cling to that, build on that." Charlie wiped away a tear, her heart aching for Ford's pain, for Katie's hurt.

"That's what I'm trying to do. The other night—when it was so healing, so 'us'—then it was suddenly as if the bridge we've built has me frozen. I'm terrified of heights and reeling with vertigo. A free fall is next," Katie said.

Her friends stood with her, arms still linked around her in support.

"I don't have any answers, but I know real love will find a way if you let it. Cliché or not, it's true," Charlie said, Jill nodding in agreement. "We've both been there, and you've been there before, too."

Jill's phone chimed and she checked the text to find a picture of Nash, bare chested, clad only in shorts on their bed, his grin suggestive. Showing it to Charlie and Katie, she said, "He'll have to wait, poor guy."

Katie shook her head. "It's okay, let's go get some rest." With that, they decided to head home for warm beds and even warmer men.

"Are you sure you're okay for now, Katie?" Charlie asked as they retrieved their shoes at the sand's edge.

Katie nodded, "It's enough that we talked, the work is up to me—and Ford."

They joined together in a last, fierce group hug before parting ways for the night.

Katie let out a breath of relief. Secret safe. She walked across the park, her steps quickening as the porch of the little blue house came into view, Ford sitting on the steps in the dim light. Even with all they had to work through, Katie was still thankful that he was home safely.

"Hey," she greeted him, frowning at his bowed head, his hand rubbing his neck. "Headache?"

Ford shrugged, scrubbing his hands over his face and raising his head to look at her. The stricken look in his eyes set off warning bells in her head. "What is it?"

Clearing his throat, Ford looked away, out to the sea. "I lost it with the kids."

"What do you mean you lost it?" Katie glanced at the darkened house reflexively, squashing her urge to run inside and check on them.

"The damn lizard got loose, the puppy went ballistic, both girls were hysterical, sure that the puppy was going to eat the lizard, Owen was screaming at them to shut up and I just...I flipped shit." He gripped his hair with both hands, head bowed.

"Nobody makes it through parenting without losing it sometimes, Ford." Katie darted another look at the door, needing to check on her babies.

His voice was ragged and barely audible. "Their faces, Katie. Miri's eyes were horrified, like I'd keeled over dead in front of her. Scarlett ran under the bed in their room, Miri joined her—both still there last I saw—and Owen took a battle stance between me and them, all fierce and scared."

"Let me go check on them, okay? They're military kids, Ford, they've been warned about such things. Sure they got scared, but don't be too hard on yourself." Katie squeezed his arm and went into the house.

CHAPTER TWENTY-EIGHT

HOW BLIND HE'D BEEN. How selfish. How goddamned selfish.

Tying his shoes, Ford left the house quietly in the pre-dawn twilight. He hoped this morning's run would enable him to gather the courage to do the only thing he knew to do to help his wife, help Miri and the rest of his family.

* * *

"Thanks so much, Ms. Lin, I appreciate it." Katie handed the bakery bag across the counter to one of her favorite and most loyal customers.

"We're so glad you're here, Katie. Those pies keep my Lin poking about the kitchen from time to time, stealing a kiss." The older lady winked at Katie as she took the bag and left the store with a cheery wave.

Sliding a tray of cookies into the front case, Reggie laughed. "You'd think after fifty-some-odd years, she wouldn't want him underfoot."

"They amaze me," Katie agreed.

Katie thought about that, about how having Ford underfoot had never been an issue for her. She'd always loved it when he'd come into the kitchen, to offer a hand, to tease and laugh, wrangle the wee beasties. Despite her determination to keep him at arm's length—when he wasn't breaking down her defenses with his kisses and those broad shoulders she loved to run her hands over—Katie was realizing that with him in close proximity, her secret couldn't last for long. She couldn't keep it—even though it meant she'd lose Ford...again.

A shadow fell from the light in the bakery's back window as the door opened. Looking up in question, Katie saw Ford step inside, taking his time in deliberately closing the door behind him. Her welcoming smile faded as she got a good look at his bleak expression. The lines bracketing his eyes were cut deep today; his hair, damp from a recent shower, stood on end where he'd clearly been repeatedly dragging his hands through it.

"Ford?" She moved a couple of steps and stopped at his raised hand, a key held between two of his fingers.

"I've got a room at the B&B. I've already dropped my gear there." His voice was oddly flat. Sucking in a breath, he pocketed the key, not looking at her.

"What?" To say she was confused would be putting it mildly.

"I'm so sorry, Katie." He looked at her now, the anguish in his eyes intense. His voice was rough yet quiet. "I'm sorry for everything. Everything then and for—for terrifying the kids, for causing you more pain over and over by refusing to leave like you want."

"Ford, the kids are okay, we talked."

He held up both hands and backed into the door, reaching behind him for the knob. "All I want is for you and the kids to be happy. If that means living apart, then—" With a helpless shrug, his hands upturned, he turned and went out the door.

Shocked, Katie stood where she was. After a moment, she blinked and looked around, unsure of what exactly had just happened.

As his words sank in, her temper flared. "How dare he." Even with an oven going, a special order spread on the counter, and a bakery full of customers out front with Reggie, Katie started to go after him. Hand on the door, she stopped. In the middle of his anger, he'd hear nothing she said anyway, even if she could catch up to him. "Damn him. Damn, damn, damn him," she muttered, stomping to the counter to snatch up her phone. She called him only to have it predictably go unanswered. Stabbing out the letters, she texted him. *Get your ass back here.*

No reply came. Again, predictably.

Channeling her fury, Katie called Nash. This abrupt change in Ford's demeanor was a red flag for anybody, much less a soldier fresh off the field and suffering from blinding post-concussive migraines. Calling her bluff about moving out or not, she needed eyes on her husband. Right now.

* * *

From his seat against the massive rock, facing the sea, Ford watched them approach like some kind of damn rescue squad. When Nash was close enough, Ford snarled and pointed, waving his finger to include all three of them. "No."

Gabe held up the water bottles in his hands. "Thought you might be thirsty."

Luke moved to lean against another rock. "I've always liked this place. Brought a girl here once for a picnic. Okay, several girls, same picnic."

Nash dropped to the rocks beside Ford with a grunt. "I needed some time off, anyway, Ford." He sat back and crossed his legs at the ankle.

Ford drained one of the water bottles Gabe passed to him and opened the second one. "Three fucking musketeers on an intervention?" he scoffed, wiping his mouth with the back of his hand.

Gabe inclined his head from where he stood a few feet away, his shades resting atop his head. "Just needed eyes on you, Ace."

"Needed space. Which is not happening, apparently." Ford glared at the three of them in turn.

"You run all the way here?" Nash asked incredulously. The cove they were currently in was at least ten miles from Main Street—and not an easy ten miles.

"No, he flew like fucking Peter Pan. Damn, Nash." Luke shook his head.

Leaving the half-assed comic relief to the other two, Gabe stepped forward and squatted low, bringing himself to eye level with Ford's face.

Shades in place, Ford's expression was inscrutable except for the sardonic twist of his mouth.

Tapping a finger next to his own eye, Gabe waited.

With a disgusted grunt, Ford pulled the shades off, glared at the other man for a full five seconds, then replaced them.

Satisfied, Gabe dropped to sit on the ground.

"I'm in no mood for touchy-feely talk," Ford warned.

"Oh, hell, no," Luke agreed, Nash shuddering for effect.

Ford brought his legs up to rest his arms on his knees, scrubbing his hands over his face. He desperately wished the other three men away—again.

Nash pulled out his phone and sent a text, getting a nearly instant answer and replying to it.

"There. Katie knows you're safe." He slanted an accusing look Ford's way. "She was pretty freaked out."

Ford growled and pushed to his feet. Enough. "Go. Away."

Gabe also stood, putting out a hand to grip Ford's arm. "See you at the bar when you're done." It wasn't a question.

Ford met the other man's steady gaze, seeing the ultimatum there, giving one of his own right back. "I'm on shift in an hour." With that he turned and resumed his run.

Nash protested, "Ford—"

"Let him go. He'll show up on shift," Luke said, pulling the Jeep keys from his pocket.

"It's gonna piss me off if I'm out looking for his sorry ass tonight instead of in bed with my wife," Nash muttered, following Gabe and Luke down to where the Jeep waited.

CHAPTER TWENTY-NINE

THE COOL, QUIET ROOM at the B&B fairly screamed with emptiness when Ford closed the door behind him with a booted foot. After a long afternoon shift filled with call after call, the bed should have been calling to him but instead the room echoed loudly. Shucking off his boots and grimy clothes, leaving them where they fell, Ford headed for the shower. Standing under the hottest water he could get, he leaned into the wall, head bowed against the spray, and remembered another day he'd felt such emptiness. The day he read the email where Katie had told him she was leaving their home and moving to the island. She'd told him where he could find them and clearly expected him to come at some point, but he knew it went much deeper than the mere relocation of his family. The email had sat unread for several weeks before he'd opened it. Once he'd read it, Ford had gone straight to the airport to board the first of several flights that would take him to his family.

Now, drying off before dropping onto the bed, the last coherent thought he had before exhaustion and headache forced him into sleep was that, if the happiest days were behind them, hopefully the kids would remember those days and survive their parents' stupidity.

CHAPTER THIRTY

AS USUAL, PANDEMONIUM REIGNED the evening as baths were splashed through, the puppy chased down—again—and snacks passed around, again. Sitting on a stool at the kitchen counter, Katie dipped a cookie in her coffee, smiling as Scarlett followed suit with her cup of milk. The girls were sitting atop the counter in front of Katie, a tea party set spread around them.

"Where's Dad?" Owen asked, closing the puppy up in his crate for the night. He'd sleep with the boy before long, but right now the wee beastie was far too rowdy at night if not contained. Owen leaned on the counter beside his mother and joined his sisters in polishing off the cookie jar's contents.

"He's working." Katie knew he was, in fact, on call according the schedule he'd sent to her phone earlier in the week. She hadn't yet figured out what to tell the kids about Ford staying at the B&B.

"He's gone away?" Scarlett's lip quivered.

Miri's eyes went wide. "What?"

"No, no, girls. Remember I told you Daddy's working with Luke on the rescue squad now? You'll see him tomorrow." She brushed back Scarlett's curls, the deep nutbrown the exact shade and texture of her father's hair.

"Do we need to talk more about what happened last night?" Katie asked. She'd gone inside to check on the kids after talking to Ford, finding them all three asleep in Owen's bed. This morning, Miri had asked if their father was okay, and they'd all seemed content to go on about the day after her reassurances that he was.

"Daddy was just a little scared." Scarlett repeated the words Owen had told her the night before. She looked at her mother for reassurance.

Katie nodded. Before she could say any more, Miri spoke up. "It's like Gabe told us. Sometimes Daddy will be nervous because he's still being a soldier and protecting us." Chewing her lip, Miri hugged her mother.

"You know he would never hurt you, right?" Katie looked at each face in turn.

"Of course he wouldn't, Mom. He'd hurt someone who tried to hurt us, though. And—" Owen looked pointedly at his sisters, "He wouldn't leave again after he promised not to. No more Army, he's home to stay now."

"Really, Mommy? Did he move here like we did?" Miriam asked.

"Really, babies, Daddy is all yours. Like most daddies, he'll be working, just not for the Army anymore. Ready to go read awhile?" Katie brushed cookie crumbs from her hands and stood, swinging Scarlett down to the floor. She handed Miriam the tea party things to put in the sink and put the lid on the cookie jar.

"Owen, can we read in your tent?" Scarlett asked, rummaging through a basket of books by the couch.

With a clearly put-upon sigh, her brother picked up his own book and pointed to the back door. "Okay, let's go."

With shrieks of excitement, the girls gathered up pillows and books to take out to the backyard. Owen and Ford had practiced their survival skills by repeatedly erecting and dismantling a four-man tent, timing themselves over and over. They'd left the tent up at Owen's request the last time. The girls had begged their brother to let them sleep out there with him, but so far he'd been adamant it was boy territory. He knew that would only fly for so long, so with a sidelong glance at his mother, he set the puppy free and followed his sisters out.

Katie smothered a smile at her son's annoyance. Ten-year-old boys were fun, so big yet still little. As she wiped down the counter, Katie fervently hoped she wouldn't be telling the kids that, while they'd see their father every day, he wouldn't be living here with them. She had no idea what was going on in Ford's head and no idea how to go about reaching him after pushing him away time and again. He'd evenly resisted her pointed hints to move out of the house up until now and this turn on a dime had her baffled.

Scooping up her phone, Katie went outside, taking a picture of the kids sprawled with their books, the tent doors tied back, two lanterns lighting the interior. She texted the shot to Ford, despite the fact that her previous two texts had gone without response. To her surprise, her phone chimed with a reply within seconds.

I'll come by and say goodnight. What did you tell them?

That you're working.

Good call. Be right there.

Relieved that she'd lay eyes on him for herself, Katie topped off her coffee, filling a second mug and carrying both outside. She turned off the light and settled at the table, propping her bare feet in a chair. Cupping her hands around her mug, she breathed deeply of the night air, feeling her shoulders unkink as her feet ached with relief to be off duty.

"Hi, Mommy!" Scarlett waved, her grin bright. Katie smiled and wiggled her fingers in response.

She felt him as soon as he stepped from the house behind her, his freshly-showered scent wrapping around her senses. He stopped next to her, the heat from his body making her clasp her hands to keep from reaching out to touch him. Scolding herself, she reached out anyway, resting a hand at his lower back. He didn't move away, relaxing his stance into her touch.

"I wondered how long it would take them to wear him down." His chuckle was wry. "Poor fella didn't have a chance, did he?"

Katie smiled. "He's a good big brother so, no, never did." She gestured to the coffee mug on the table, accepting his brief smile of thanks with a nod. He sat next to her, sipping coffee and watching the girls chatter and show each other book pages, Owen intently reading his own book despite the constant jostling.

The night breeze ruffled her hair, and the kids' voices mingled with the sounds of laughter drifting on the air from the street.

"Come home, Ford," she said quietly, touching his fingers where his hand wrapped around the mug he'd returned to the table.

His sigh was deep and long. "We tried that."

Her sigh matched his. "I know I've pushed you not to stay here, but things have changed—haven't they?"

He cleared his throat, his hands tightening on his cup. "I thought they had."

Before Katie could ask him to clarify, Owen spied his father.
"Hey, Dad!"

Shrieks from both girls followed as they ran to cling to their father's legs. Ford walked to the tent with a girl on each leg, shaking off first one then the other before he crouched down to crawl inside. Wrestling his son with one arm, he fended off the puppy with the other while the girls climbed over his back. He settled them all by opening a book and beginning to read aloud, his deep baritone commanding attention easily.

Katie watched them, hoping the scene was helping patch the cracks inside him, helping him see that right here was where he belonged. It had taken her a while to believe in them again, and, in the painful process of her lessons, she feared she'd taught him the opposite.

The radio he'd laid on the table crackled to life, summoning Ford from the cozy tangle of kids. Extricating himself gingerly, he tucked the blanket around his now drowsy daughters and tousled his son's hair.

"All secure," Owen said, mirroring Ford's smile.

"Come back later? Talk with me?" Katie held out the radio, holding onto it for a beat until he spared her a glance.

Their gaze held, conveying so much, leaving so much unsaid. Katie released the radio and watched him jog away.

CHAPTER THIRTY-ONE

KATIE WAS AMAZED that the days went by as if her world hadn't imploded with fresh uncertainty, fear and anger. Kids were tended to, the bakery ran as usual, the sun shone, the waves moved to and fro as they had for eons and would for eons more. As much as she was relieved for the space from Ford, she was even more relieved he continued to show up to spend time with the kids around his shifts, taking them to the beach, to the big town on the mainland so they could show him around, to get ice cream and coming by every night at bedtime if he wasn't out on a call. She managed to avoid him just about every time by retreating to the bakery or for a walk on the beach, sometimes alone, other times with Jill or Charlie or both. Jane had managed to get away to join them a couple of times recently. Listening to her dish about her budding romance with Luke had been fun.

With the bakery closed that day, Katie sat on the porch in the morning sun, Scarlett playing with her tiny dolls on the steps. Ford had shown up early to take Owen and Miri fishing along with Amos, Gabe and Rory. Amos loved his fishing spot at the edge of a quiet cove just below his house. He could still get there easily on his own, as Gabe had made sure to keep the boardwalk and railing leading down from the old man's house in good shape. Ford had made it a habit to drop in on his grandfather-in-law and cast a line with him often. Owen, Miri and Rory did the same, ensuring that Amos had plenty of company on the days he didn't want anyone to bring him down to Katie's or to The Painted Parrot.

* * *

Ford sat back in his chair, his fishing rod loosely in hand, a sharp ear on the kids baiting their hooks and casting their lines down the cove's beach a little ways. Amos's sigh of contentment brought a smile to Ford's face. Meeting Gabe's eyes over the old man's head, he nodded, knowing the other man's thoughts. More of this would happen. What was an island life if you couldn't make more time for fishing?

"You know, I caught the island's biggest blue marlin about ten years ago, right here. I don't know how he got in this cove, but he was the gran'pappy of 'em all. Nobody has seen him since." Amos whittled on a palm-sized piece of wood, his two fishing rods leaned against forked poles stuck in the sand on either side of him. He eyeballed the lines closely before returning to the wood, which was beginning to take shape beneath his hands.

"Let him go?" Ford asked, clearly surprised.

Gabe laughed with Amos, winking at the old man. "He's a soldier, but we'll make him a fisherman yet."

Amos slapped Ford's shoulder, the knife expertly tucked safely aside in his hand. "Sure I let him go. Nobody should tame a beast like that. He'd earned his way, plus had years of procreation to go yet. I do wonder from time to time if he's lazing about his last days down there somewhere." Amos gazed out into the smooth glass of the cove waters.

"He probably found his happy hunting ground racing sharks and chasing off dolphins years ago," Gabe said, also looking out on the water, but with a sudden stillness that snapped Ford alert.

Following Gabe's line of sight, Ford saw a small boat almost hidden in the trees at the edge of the cove's other shore. If not for the fading yellow paint catching the sun, they might not have even seen the craft. With a lift of his chin at Ford, Gabe rose from his chair into a stretch.

"Fancy a walkabout, Ace?" Gabe said casually.

"You might check out that east shore. There's been a light bobbling about over there now and again," Amos said, idly readjusting his pole.

"Why didn't you let me know, you old geezer?" Gabe asked.

"If I had to call one of you boys for every little thing out here, I'd have moved to town years ago," Amos grumbled. Pointing to a faded army green backpack under his chair. "I'm armed and I know what's what."

Gabe agreed. "Yeah, you do. Seen anything specific?"

Amos shook his head. "I wouldn't let the kids run as far amok as usual, but I haven't seen anybody. Probably a good idea to do a drive by in the boat from time to time, let whoever's out there know we've got an eye or two out."

"Hey, Owen," Ford called out. Owen anchored his pole in the sand and ran to Ford's side.

"Need help with your pole, Dad?" The boy grinned.

"Funny kid," Ford laughed, tousling his son's perpetually unruly hair. "Gabe and I are going to check a few things out over on the east side, you and the girls stay put with Papa until we get back."

Owen eyed his father's face, eyebrow raised, knowing something was up because rarely were the kids reined in from running amok on the island.

Ford dropped his voice low, "We need to check something out, keep 'em close."

The sense of being trusted to look out for others straightened Owen's ten-year-old shoulders with pride. Nodding conspiratorially, he went back to his pole and casually moved to set up his spot a ways past Miri and Rory, effectively boxing them in between himself and Amos.

Ford sent the boy a two-fingered salute, and got one plus a grin in return. He clapped a hand to Amos's shoulder and jogged to catch up as Gabe disappeared around the bend that would lead them to the other side of the cove. Neither man was particularly worried, but some things warranted a closer look—especially since the partially hidden boat was solidly on Amos's property. While islanders came and went freely, hiding a boat was a point of curiosity if not concern.

"I'm not liking the look of this," Ford commented a few minutes later, squatting beside what appeared to be campfire remnants, cigarette butts and junk food trash among the ashes and leaves. He moved things around with a finger, dislodging more bits of trash. "Seems like if it was just a random islander they wouldn't have left a mess."

Gabe pointed a finger at the other man. "Exactly. Islanders would never leave a mess behind. Even tourists usually clean up decently around here, as they're typically nature lovers. We have a few ramblers or hermits, but I've never known them to do something like this. This just isn't the kind of place that gets trashed."

Both men walked further, scanning both the ground and the surrounding trees. Walking out of the woods into the sun again, Ford pulled his shades back down.

After a quick look around to be sure they were alone, Gabe strode to the partially hidden boat. Hands in his pockets, he leaned in to examine the hull that stuck out from the branches. "BessieJo." He read the fading blue paint. "Oh, hey. This is an old skiff of Amos's. I haven't seen it in years."

"Wonder why it's all the way out here. He hasn't been this far on his own in ages, has he?" Ford walked back into the trees, circling around the boat's hiding place.

"I wouldn't think so. And I know it wasn't here last time we came fishing because it wasn't that hard to spot, but also look at these fresh breaks." Gabe pulled out his phone to snap a couple of pictures of the boat and the crushed branches around it. You never knew.

"Take a look at this." Gabe followed Ford's voice, joining him in the trees behind the boat.

Seeing a small stash of canned food, bottled water and a camo backpack under the boat, both men automatically moved to grid scan the area. Finding nothing else, Gabe took a few more pictures and sent them with a text of explanation to Luke. "We'll get Luke to come poke around. Likely a new wanderer hoping to get just lost enough out here for a while, but we'll be sure."

Ford nodded his agreement, and the two men made their way back across the cove.

"I heard you gave your drinking business to the bar in town last night." Gabe knew he was probably skirting busybody status, but he cared a lot about Katie and the kids and had come to care about Ford as well. No matter how wild the waves, nobody sank on his watch.

Ford stopped walking and turned to face Gabe, pushing up his shades to meet the other man's eyes. "I just needed space to check out without being alone or being rescued."

Gabe also pushed up his shades, his gaze unwavering. "You'll call me next time." It wasn't a question.

Ford squinted and replaced his shades, rubbing his forehead as he did so. "Won't be a next time, but yeah."

The rest of the short walk back to Amos's dock was silent, both men lost in their thoughts while scanning about for anything odd.

"Amos, that was your old skiff we found. You been out and about?" Gabe asked the old man, taking up the chair next to him.

"The BessieJo hasn't been seaworthy in years," Amos mused, his voice dropping off as his head dipped forward onto his chest.

Gabe glanced at his phone screen. "Luke says he'll be out shortly if we want to wait around and look further with him."

Ford settled back into the wooden Adirondack style chair and tipped his ball cap over his eyes. "Let's fish, then."

Gabe's laugh echoed as he stretched out his legs and mirrored the other man's pose, the kids chattering nearby and Amos's light snores blending with the birdsong and occasional splash out in the water.

CHAPTER THIRTY-TWO

SMILING AT THE CHORUS of "Hey, Mommy!" and "Hey, Katie!", Katie joined the group already on the beach, chasing Scarlett knee deep into the sea and swinging her high, showering them with droplets of water that sparkled in the sun. If nothing else, the kids, the sun and sea could be depended upon to work their soothing magic.

When Scarlett scampered off to catch crabs and build sand houses for them, Katie dropped to the sand next to where Jill was building a sand...something with Zane. At her curious look, Jill lifted her hands. "I'm not the architect here."

Zane crowed cheerfully, plopping a cup of sand atop the pile, his little feet immediately destroying any semblance of structure.

"You okay?" Jill asked.

Charlie, settled in a nearby lounge chair, looked up from her book to smile at Katie.

Katie shrugged, scooping sand into a bright blue cup. "I've no idea what I am."

"Ma, look!" Rory called to Charlie, gesturing to a nearly foot-tall sandcastle adorned with shells and sea glass.

"Beautiful!" Charlie called back. To Katie and Jill she said, "Rory asked me awhile back if she could call me Ma, that she didn't think her Mommy would mind. My heart melted, I tell you, just melted."

"Awww," Jill said, feeling a special connection with the girl she'd gone with Gabe to bring home when he'd learned of her existence. He and Charlie had just been getting to know each other at the time.

"That's so sweet," Katie replied. "I know how hard it is to lose a mother when you're young. I'm so glad she has you and Gabe."

Before she could think too far back in her memories, Katie looked at the sandcastles. "Island kids perfect the art of sandcastle building early, don't they?"

Jill skeptically eyed the pile of sand in front of Zane, who gleefully smashed his red cup into it again. "If you say so."

Katie couldn't help but laugh, leaning over to smooch the top of the baby's head and ending up with a lap full of sandy baby. The day was brighter just being there.

Katie sighed deeply, turning the baby to sit in his sand pile again.

"We're listening," Charlie said gently.

"We're just living day to day, moment by moment. Steering clear of each other, mostly." Katie reached up to redo her ponytail. "What gets me the most is that one night. For the first time, it felt like we just might have a chance. It was so damn good. Holding him and being held by him, it was as if I could finally breathe. As if being in his arms was what I needed to put all the pieces back together. Then he left me—again—only this time it's my fault." Katie threw her hands up and let them fall.

Just then Charlie's phone rang, and, since it was Gabe's ringtone, she smiled apologetically at Katie as she answered it.

"Hey. Oh, no. Where? I'll send her. Love you." Charlie ended the call and stood up. "Katie, it's Amos. At your house. Go, we've got the kids."

Katie scrambled to her feet, calling out to the kids, "Stay with Charlie, I'll be back soon."

"My house?" she asked Charlie as she returned her friend's tight hug, found her shoes and took off at a run.

"That's what Gabe said." Charlie chewed her lip, arm in arm with Jill as they watched their friend go.

Katie ran across the park, now hearing the sirens as the First Responders arrived. Gabe must have heard the call go out and called Charlie immediately.

As she hit the street in front of her house, Katie saw Ford's Jeep parked askew in her yard, doors open, and the island ambulance in her driveway. Luke and Ford were kneeling on the ground at the foot of her porch steps, she could see Amos's booted feet between the two men.

Above Amos's head, Tag slipped a soft restraint collar on him, talking calmly to him while the other two men worked.

At her approach, neither man looked up from their work, but Amos's faded blue met hers. "Just a little spill, Katiegirl, no need for all this fuss." Her grandfather's words were much more reassuring than his wavering voice, his crooked smile trying to reassure her as she knelt and took his hand.

Next to her, Ford bandaged a nasty cut on the old man's forehead while, across from him, Luke got an IV line going.

Leaning in close, Katie brought Amos's hand to her cheek. "What happened, Papa?" While her focus was on Amos, she was keenly aware of the warmth of Ford's body against her side, aware of how safe he made her feel. She watched his hands as he worked, his forearms flexing, so strong yet his touch on Amos's face so gentle.

Luke smiled at her, taping the IV line in place. "The man says he stumbled on the steps. We'll get him checked out."

Amos grumbled about bossy men who were just boys yesterday, but there was no sting to his words. Even Katie could see his color was pale and his breathing erratic as, once on the gurney, he finally let his eyes close.

"I'll be right behind the ambulance, Papa," Katie told him, tucking his hand under the sheet Luke spread over him.

Amos squeezed her hand as Tag and Luke lifted the gurney and rolled it to the waiting ambulance doors.

* * *

Ford straightened from repacking the gear bag and cleaning up the site. His heart had nearly stopped when the call had come across his radio for this address. With three kids and a wife, there were a million scenarios that had rushed through his mind. When the dispatcher said the victim in question was Amos and he was alone, Ford's first thought had been to wonder why Amos was there alone.

Katie brushed errant hair strands behind her ears and clasped her hands at the back of her head. "What on earth was he doing here? Did he walk all the way from home? Was it just a stumble or did something else cause the fall?" Covering her face with her hands for a beat, Katie took a fortifying breath. "I'll get my keys."

Before she could push past him to go into the house, Ford held out a hand, raising his voice to be heard over the ambulance siren as it moved down the street, "Let me take you."

When she hesitated, her eyes wounded and wary, he added, "Please. You don't need to drive right now."

"Is that the ace med evac's opinion?" she shot out, pulling out her phone to text Jill an update. She growled in frustration as her fingers shook too much to finish the text, confirming his opinion about her driving right now. Marching past him to climb into the open door of his Jeep, she slammed the door closed, buckled up and sat fuming. After the past few days, to be thrust into his presence like this was just too much.

Ford swung the gear bag into the back seat. "Yes, it is my medical opinion—as your husband." Jerking into gear, the Jeep sped off, following the ambulance's path.

Katie scoffed, "Said *husband* isn't currently starring in that role at the moment." Crossing her arms, she put on her shades and settled in for the ride.

With wisdom he didn't know he'd learned, Ford closed his mouth and stayed that way for the duration of the ride across the island.

He glanced at her from time to time as he drove, the wind whipping her ponytail, the sun glinting off her shades. Her face remained impassive, a tear smeared at edge of her sunglasses. Just looking at her made something slip around his heart and squeeze so tightly he lost breath. He had no idea how they could go forward from this—how they each could forgive being shut out the way they had.

Once at the hospital, Katie rushed inside after Amos, refusing to spare Ford a single glance.

At the ER desk, Luke finished the paperwork and turned to Ford, leaning next to him. "You're still on shift, but let me ask back up to stay on so you can stay nearby. She's going to need you."

"Thanks," Ford said.

Luke nodded, clapping a hand to Ford's shoulder and heading for the door. "You know where to find me."

Ford strode down the hall in search of Katie. He certainly didn't intend to walk away and leave her to face this alone.

CHAPTER THIRTY-THREE

FORD FOUND KATIE in an ER cubicle holding Amos's hand while the old man dozed, the machines around him beeping and whirring. Her head resting against the railing, Katie's eyes were closed, her lips moving slightly in words Ford knew were likely a prayer. While never a church goer, she'd discovered prayer early in their marriage. He'd always suspected it was largely the result of his habit of flying into war zones all the time, but they'd never talked about it. Knowing that about her warmed him a little as he stepped into the cubicle, drawing the curtain closed behind him.

Hearing him, Katie stirred, opening her eyes, but keeping them on Amos's motionless form.

"Whatever you need, I'm here." He reached out to touch her hand where it gripped the bed rail, her knuckles white.

She drew back, tucking the hand in her lap. "You can't have it both ways, Ford."

He sighed, running a hand through his hair, jamming both hands in his pockets.

"The episodes make me useless, plus you've been asking for space..." Ford let his voice trail away. He fingered the key in his pocket. How could a decision be so right yet so wrong?

"What do you need? The bakery? The kids? Coffee?"

He was rewarded as her head turned at that last one, a hopeful expression on her face.

He chuckled. "Ah, yes. Be right back." He squeezed her shoulder as he left the cubicle, his touch leaving a warm spot.

*   *   *

Thankful for the reprieve, Katie stood to stretch and pace the room. Her grandfather looked so weak and small lying there. His vital signs were stable now, that was something. Rubbing her neck against the feeling of unease that was tightening down, Katie worried over Amos. Why had he been at the house with no one home? While the door was always open to Amos, his habit was to call her or someone else for a ride. Was his fall down the steps just a fall, or had something caused it? The questions swirled about in her mind as Amos's personal physician arrived, waking his patient when he opened the curtain.

With a reassuring smile to Katie, Dr. Talbot assessed his patient with shrewd eyes. "Acrobatics on the steps, Amos?"

Amos waved a hand in the air. "Missed a step is all, young man. Much to do about nothing, these kids."

Dr. Talbot performed his exam in short order, having already read the intake notes from both the EMTs and the ER nurses. "You know what I'm going to say, Amos. I'd like to admit you and run a few tests."

The old man grimaced, shifting to sit up in the bed. Katie moved to his side, pushing the button to raise the head of the bed for him. "I just need some coffee and a good plate of seafood gumbo."

Returning with coffee in each hand, Ford laughed. "I've no doubt Jill will hear about that and fix you right up." He handed Katie one of the coffee cups, which she held up to her face, breathing in the scent deeply before sipping. He leaned in close, so close she felt the warmth radiate from his body. "Junkie," he whispered.

Rolling her eyes, Katie turned her attention back to the doctor. "Tests?" she prompted, as the doctor had fallen silent while he looked over the computer screen next to Amos's bed.

"Yes. There are few things that concern me, and further tests will help determine if that concern is valid." The doctor finished typing his orders and turned back to his patient. "We'll get you settled upstairs in better comfort, Amos. Get you more pillows and a TV remote." He patted the old man's leg and left the room, Katie on his heels. Ford stayed by Amos's bedside, distracting him with baseball talk. They'd recently discovered a mutual fatal attraction for Cubs baseball that hadn't waned for either of them despite years of distance.

Down the hall, the doctor turned to Katie, his voice gentle. "There's no point in speculating, Katie. Let's get him settled comfortably and see what the tests tell us. We'll talk in the morning."

Thanking him, Katie turned to rejoin her grandfather and Ford. She paused a few feet away from the cubicle, listening to the two of them talk. Stepping quietly closer so she could see them before they saw her, she watched the two men she loved so much. They were still talking baseball, Ford standing next to Amos's bedside, his stance relaxed and open. While she watched, Ford threw back his head and laughed in the way she'd seen him do often with the kids. Cradling the coffee cup in her hands, the warmth soothing, she stepped into the room.

"Katiegirl, no need for the two of you to hover. Go do things, come back later," Amos tried again with his granddaughter.

Katie gave him an eye with an expression he recognized as futile to argue with. Her grandmother and her mother had often given him that exact expression over the years. The thought made the old man smile as he closed his eyes to hold on to those images in his mind.

As Amos drifted off, Katie stretched her arms above her head and rolled her neck. With practiced ease, Ford reached out to rub her neck.

Katie moaned when his thumbs hit just behind her ears: he knew all the perfect spots to hit, always had. As she let her head drop forward, his fingers strong and soothing, Ford's voice was in her ear.

"What can I do, Katiebean? The bakery? The kids? More coffee?" His slight chuckle at the end brought a reluctant smile to her face. Raising her head and stepping away from him, Katie shook her head. "Reggie already has the bakery under control, the kids are with Jill and Charlie." She saluted him with her coffee cup to indicate there was plenty left.

"Since he's stable and likely won't have tests until tomorrow, why don't you go get some rest? Let me handle getting the kids?"

With a sigh, Katie sat in the plastic chair in the corner. "Ford, we can't ignore things, despite this turn of events." She waved a hand in Amos's direction.

Ford paced the small space, raising his hands in the air and dropping them.

Before he could reply, the machines went haywire. Katie jumped to her feet, at his side immediately. "Papa, what is it?"

Amos's hands fluttered about, one going to his chest, the other reaching for Katie. The room exploded with activity, nurses dashing in and issuing rapid-fire questions and orders. Resisting the nurse aide's attempt to move them into the hallway, Katie stood against the wall, her hands over her mouth. With a hand on the nurse aide's arm, Ford stepped into Katie's line of sight, blocking the scene in front of her. Frowning, Katie tilted her head, keeping her eyes on the the professionals working on her grandfather while she tried to push Ford aside. Using his size to his advantage, Ford again stepped into her line of vision, his hands on her arms, and steered her into the hallway.

Turning her head to try and see Amos, Katie pushed at his hands, her grip desperate and clawing. "Let me go, damn you!" Her voice was shrill, her eyes wild.

Ford sat down in a chair and pulled her into his lap, anchoring her there with his arms around her. "Katie. Hey, hey, look at me, look." Dipping his head, he met her eyes as she turned to face him, keeping his arms in place, effectively trapping her.

"Ford Callahan, if you don't—" Katie broke off, her fist against her mouth.

Ford held tight. "I've got you."

Wrapped in Ford's arms, his body surrounding her, was both calming and infuriating. Katie fought to control her wild emotions, made wilder by this man who filled her senses in every way.

"I can't lose Amos now, oh God, I can't," she whispered brokenly. "He's the only one who won't let me down." Her words were like darts to Ford's heart, again driving home the point that not only could he not fix it for her, but that she wouldn't let him if he could. He desperately wanted to roar and run far away, outside of these walls, away from things he couldn't fix. But he wouldn't—not this time. A slight tremor ran through his body, but Katie was oblivious to it, absorbed in her worry for her grandfather.

While the medical team worked on Amos, Katie curled her fingers into her husband's shirt and held on, letting him shield her from everything for just this moment. It felt so good to be held, to hold on to him amid the storm. He was so solid and strong. This is how it should have been then, she couldn't help but think.

Suddenly, right there in the hospital hallway, it all clicked into place with stark clarity. It was painfully clear to her that even if Ford hadn't shut her out, even if he would have let the Army fly him home, he couldn't have stood with her through her own ordeal. He'd have been in a hospital bed himself, out of his mind with his own pain. Completely unable to be there for her. Her Fix-It Man would have been in a rage of helplessness—in fact, he had been just that all those miles away. He'd told her so the other night. Suddenly his perspective was clear to her—why that was happening now, she'd never know—and it made all the difference.

"Oh, Ford." She let loose of his shirt and sat up straight. "Ford, I'm so sorry—"

Her words were cut off as members of the medical team trickled out from Amos's cubicle, the curtain opening for Dr. Talbot.

Ford released her and stood with her, taking her hand in his as she stepped forward to meet the doctor.

"We've got him stabilized—all is well for now. He'll likely rest deeply for a while," the doctor told her.

"What happened?" Katie looked past the doctor to her grandfather's bed where he lay, the sheets smooth and white.

"His blood pressure suddenly nosedived, sending him into a tailspin, but he's stable now. Let's get him moved upstairs, and I'll be in to talk further."

The doctor walked away, leaving more questions than answers, in Ford's opinion.

Katie rushed to her grandfather's side, leaning over to kiss his cheek. "Amos, don't you ever do that again," she admonished in a whisper, resting her forehead against his.

Two orderlies came in, telling her Amos was being moved up to a room. "He'll be all settled in just a few, ma'am," one of them told her while the other one handed her a paper with the room number on it. "They'll text you when he's admitted, if you'd step around to the desk and finish up the paperwork in the meantime."

Thanking them, Katie watched the two men wheel Amos's bed away, Ford standing close at her side.

"I'll go do the paperwork if you want to follow them." Ford squeezed her shoulders.

"Thanks." Katie walked quickly to catch up to Amos' side.

CHAPTER THIRTY-FOUR

RIDING THE ELEVATOR back up to Amos's room later that afternoon, Katie sipped her coffee, hoping the double-shot afternoon jolt would keep her going full speed ahead for a few more hours. She planned to go back to the bakery for a while before calling it a day.

Stepping into the room, Katie found the doctor there, talking earnestly with his patient. Said patient was sitting upright in the bed, clearly agitated. Amos pointed at Katie, "You tell her. I'm done talking about it with you." He pointed a finger at the doctor, his wrinkled tan face flushed with irritation. "And I'm going home today."

The doctor sighed and turned to Katie. Before he could say a word, Amos spoke up again, "And don't talk about me in here, go away." The old man sank back into the pillows, allowing Katie to help him get a sip of water. "Papa—"

Amos gripped her hand, his eyes closing in exhaustion. "Katiegirl, go talk to the doctor. Then you can take me home."

Katie squeezed his hand and followed Dr. Talbot out into the hallway.

The doctor sighed, his gaze meeting Katie's. "He's in bad shape, Katie. I don't know how much you know of his history, but today's news isn't good."

Katie clasped her hands together tightly in front of her, willing herself to stay collected. "Unfortunately, since I'm new to the scene, I know nothing. Amos has had a few of what he calls 'spells' since I got here, but I never could get him to talk about it. I've not been privy to medical information yet. I'm his next of kin, I should have checked up on it."

"It's nothing you could have changed in any way, Katie." The doctor's eyes were kind and tired. "Two things. He's had congestive heart failure for years, it's taking a toll. Then, a little over two years ago, he was diagnosed with Alzheimer's." Seeing her distress, Dr. Talbot reached out to squeeze Katie's arm.

"He's been on a treatment protocol that seems to have kept it slow progressing. He was in Stage Two when we did the assessment and diagnosis, but I believe that's changed now. I'll need to update testing before we know more at this point. We'll do that in the office next week—he's in no mood today and that's not likely to improve until he gets to go home."

Katie couldn't help but roll her eyes. "Stubborn."

The doctor nodded and continued. While he talked, Katie tried to listen, to ask the right questions, but all she could think of was how she'd only found Amos last year and arrived on the island to see him in person barely eight months ago. Her mother's daddy. And now she was losing him, just like she'd lost her mother, her father, nearly Ford. Her secret weighed heavily as she thought about how unfair it all was. Looking down at her brightly patterned shoes, it was all Katie could do not to slide to the floor and wail. But she wouldn't. She focused again on Dr. Talbot's words. "Hospice care?" Her head snapped up.

"We have a facility over on the big island or we—the team—can help you take care of him at home. I'll have my nurse connect you with information you need. You can take him home soon, but let's get him stable for a few days first. The time has come for someone to be with him around the clock. The nurse and social worker here will help create a basic plan of care with you before we discharge him." The doctor patted Katie's shoulder and briskly strode away, as if he hadn't just shaken up her world and sent everything spinning like some kind of old-fashioned pinball game. Shoot the ball and watch it all go berserk.

Having taken care of things for as long as she could remember, and being determined never to be let down again, Katie took several deep breaths, pressing her fingers against her eyes firmly. She had far too much to do to fall apart now. Just as she pushed away from the wall to reenter Amos's room, her phone chimed a text from Ford.

How's our Papa?

Reading the words across the screen brought home the reminder to Katie that she didn't have to carry the burden alone this time.

She'd be strong, she'd handle things—but she could have help if she only allowed it. Suddenly all the exercises in strength of the past years seemed to come together in one stormy wash of emotions that swept over and around her until she couldn't breathe. But this time, this time she could have an anchor, a calm at the center of that storm where she could cling and breathe amid the fray. Where she could cling then rise to stand strong again.

Feeling her eyes prickling with tears again, she typed the words only to erase them from the screen three times. Battered by everything at once, she typed the words again and this time she hit send.

Can you come?

Before she could go back to her grandfather's room, the phone vibrated with Ford's reply.

On my way.

The relief that flooded her at his response was incredible, begetting a flood of fresh strength just when she'd thought she had no more.

Returning to Amos's side, Katie watched the old man sleep while a kaleidoscope of words tumbled about in her head. *Alzheimer's. Heart Failure. Hospice. Family. Strong. Choice. Not Alone. Love. Dying. Ford. Time. Papa. Home.*

When Ford strode in minutes later, she turned and buried her head into his neck.

Without missing a beat, his arms wrapped around her tightly. Like a child needing comfort, she folded her arms up against his chest, hands under her chin and took shelter in his embrace. Surrounded by his strength, she shut out the world, filling her senses with only him. This was becoming a habit. Her eyes closed, she breathed in his scent—brine of the sea and remnants of his woodsy soap—the sound of his soothing murmurs in her ear, the feel of his damp t-shirt against her face. After a few moments, she stepped back, her breath blowing away wayward strands of hair. "Why are you wet?"

Ford pulled the shirt away from his body with a wry grimace. "Water rescue earlier, haven't had time to change. Tell me." He took her hands in his, and his deep blue eyes filled with concern steadied her somehow.

She told him what the doctor had told her, her voice wavering a few times.

"I'm so sorry," he said quietly, still holding her hands in his.

Katie nodded. "Me, too."

Ford's radio crackled at the same time his cell phone chimed. With an apologetic wince, he turned the radio down but listened intently to the dispatch.

Listening, too, Katie squeezed his hands and dropped them. "You're needed. Go."

"I'm needed right here."

"It's just waiting now, the nurse will come talk, I'll talk with Papa and then I'll be home. You know he won't tolerate me sleeping here." Katie gave her husband a shove, walking to the door of the room with him. "Go be a hero, Ace."

With an eye roll and a muttered "Hero, she says," Ford cupped her chin and tipped her face up. "We've got this." He kissed her hard and strode down the hall, answering his radio along the way.

Katie watched him go, the apparently seawater-dampened navy blue t-shirt molded against his body, his muscles bunching as he moved. She laughed when a couple of nurses elbowed one another, gawking as he passed by. He was a sight to see, her big, handsome, fiercely intent badass.

Amos stirred, prompting her to return to his side. He didn't wake, so Katie paced the room before sitting down, pulling a notebook from her bag. "Time to make a plan, Papa," she murmured, already lost in thought with the many things she needed to think through at the moment. What to tell the kids? Where would Amos stay now that he couldn't be left alone? Her house would be easier, but just yanking him from his home wasn't fair. Would she need to take time away from the bakery to be with him 24/7—or would that come later? Her mind spun as her pen scribbled questions and options.

She spoke Ford's parting words aloud, "We've got this."

CHAPTER THIRTY-FIVE

SURROUNDED BY SUGAR COOKIES by the dozen, Katie looked up from placing chocolate candy eyes on what would soon be smiley face cookies as the bakery's back door opened. Now closed, the front of the bakery was dark while the back was ablaze with light and music.

"Big to-do?" Jill asked, eyeing the dozens of cookies around the kitchen.

"Two to-dos, I'm just lucky enough that the same cookie works for both." Katie grinned, continuing to place the candies. "Help yourself." Jill was known for popping in for a sweet treat and a chat from time to time after hours. Sometimes the kids were underfoot, sometimes it was just the two of them, and other times it grew into a girls' night complete with wine and babies falling asleep on a blanket in the corner.

"I just came by to see you for myself. Texts don't do this kind of news justice." Jill side-hugged her friend. Donning a pair of gloves, she reached into the bowl for a handful of colorful candies and joined Katie's work.

"I know. Thank you." Katie sighed. "I didn't want to leave Amos tonight. This time it's harder for him to face, I think. Two years ago he didn't have us."

"You thinking about a plan?" Finished with the cookie eyes, Jill freshened Katie's coffee cup and poured one for herself. A trauma nurse in another lifetime, she was well versed medically and knew just what they were facing—as much as anyone could know.

Filling a pastry bag with icing, Katie shrugged. "Right now all I know is that he can't live alone anymore. He was too groggy to discuss details this evening." Expertly drawing smiles on the bright yellow iced cookies, Katie made her way around the trays with efficient speed. "I wish his house was big enough, I'd just move us in with him. The thought of moving him out of his home at this point seems so unfair. It's where he's happiest and he should be where he's happiest, y'know?"

"I know." Jill nodded, adding hot, sudsy water to the sink full of dishes.

"Stop working, put your feet up," Katie nudged her friend, tossing the empty pastry bag into the soapy water.

"Ppfftt." Jill continued to wash dishes while Katie finished up for the night, the cookies needing to set before they were boxed for the morning's pickup.

"So I don't know." Katie wiped down the last counter and tossed the towel into the laundry basket by the back door. She'd put the load in to wash at home before going to bed.

Jill flipped off the bakery lights, and Katie locked up, hoisting the laundry basket to her hip as the two walked around the side of the bakery to the street.

"Thanks for coming by. Want an escort for the walk home? Ford won't mind."

Jill laughed, shaking her head. "Still a city girl." The two hugged, and Jill turned to walk across the park and down to the beach cottages. "Send the kids to the Parrot whenever you head to see Amos. I'm there til threeish," Jill called as she jogged across the road.

"I'll let ya know," Katie called back.

"Ford won't mind what?" His voice came from the depths of the darkened porch as Katie climbed the steps slowly, her body giving up the long day.

She set the basket by the door and joined him on the bench, a little groan slipping out as she sat. "I volunteered you to walk Jill home. Your lessons from our early years in the city are still in my head."

Ford chuckled, "I remember the first time I asked you not to go out alone. You looked at me like I'd lost my mind."

"Mmmhmm. I was trying to figure out whether you were overly possessive or running from something." Katie's voice held a note of amusement.

"That was our first hard-won compromise, getting you to promise me a heads up when you went out." Ford reached over to bring Katie's legs into his lap. "You acted like the phone I gave you was a leash."

Settling her legs in his lap, she lay back on the padded bench. He rubbed her legs, paying special attention to her aching calves. "At the time, I thought it was."

"I wanted to take care of you from the moment you yelled at me for spilling your coffee," he said.

"That take-out coffee was my one weekly indulgence, and I'd barely taken a sip," Katie continued their path down memory lane, her voice dropping lower as he pushed her shoes to the porch and rubbed one foot, then the other.

"If I remember correctly, I more than made it up to you," he said.

Katie let her eyes drift closed. "Yeah, by buying me that exact coffee every day for a week."

Ford went quiet as Katie stilled, her breathing deepening. Just as he laid his head back against the house, her feet still in his hands, she jolted fully awake and sat up with a gasp.

"Amos!" She frantically dug for her phone, admonishing herself in a tirade of half finished sentences.

"Hey, hey!" Ford grabbed her hands. "You don't think I would have come to get you if he needed you?"

Katie relaxed, breathless. "I can't believe I forgot."

"You didn't forget. I told you I'd check on him, and you trusted me." Ford kissed each hand and reached out to smooth back her hair. "Breathe. I took the kids to see him after supper. He was settled in for the night, seemed okay. I meant to text you when we got home but got sidetracked with bedtime shenanigans. You got some rowdy kids, lady."

"Yeah, they get that from their father." She giggled at his arched brow, his mock menacing expression familiar.

"Ford. NO." She giggled harder, springing to her feet despite her weariness. Ford was faster, pulling her to his lap, fingers mercilessly tickling her ribs. Thinking of the sleeping kids, she clapped a hand over her mouth midshriek.

"Stop it," she gasped, "You'll wake the babies."

"*I'll* wake the babies?" he whispered with a chuckle. "I'm not the one being loud."

Another shriek escaped her as he tickled afresh. "Ford. Ford, stop it. Right now." She wriggled in his arms, her shirt riding up.

He let his fingers go still for a moment, then drifted his hand across her bare belly, caressing her soft skin.

Katie froze for a moment before melting against him, seeking his lips with hers. For a badass, he had such tender, full lips. She sighed against his mouth.

"Amos can't live alone anymore."

"I know." He tightened his arms around her, resting his chin on her head. "What're you thinking?"

"I have no idea. He shouldn't have to leave his place, but it's too far up there for keeping an eye on him. I'd gladly move in there with the kids but it's practically a two-room shack, there's no room."

"Let's put you to bed, Bean. We'll sleep on it. I'm going to stay here in case you have to leave quickly for Amos." He eased away and stood, steadying her against his side with one arm, opening the screen door with the other.

Katie was asleep before her head hit the pillow, and Ford pulled the covers around her. Restless, he checked on the kids and made his way back outside, this time to lie out in the backyard. The stars might not have the answers, but they'd bring him peace while he tried to find some.

CHAPTER THIRTY-SIX

THE MORNING FOUND AMOS bright eyed and full of his usual spark, allowing Katie to return to the bakery for the day, with promises to bring him his beloved gumbo instead of hospital food when she came to see him and talk with his doctor.

The back of the bakery was hopping as usual with Miri and Rory glazing doughnuts while Owen expertly swiped a handful of doughnut holes on his way to load his bike bread basket for the morning deliveries. Katie slid a tray of her tarts into the oven and took a moment to stretch her back, watching the kids with a smile. This was exactly what she'd envisioned when she'd packed up her family and come all the way out here to the middle of the ocean. Kids underfoot in the bakery, helping and laughing. An extended family of close-knit friends. It was such a good life.

As the bell hanging from the back door rang out and Ford stepped inside, Katie sighed. And that right there was the bonus she hadn't counted on in her island dreams. He filled the back of the bakery with his presence, his dark gray rescue squad t-shirt emblazoned with bright orange, his utility belt at his waist showing he was either on duty or fresh off. She knew up close he'd smell of woodsy soap and clean, salty sweat, even above the delicious bakery smells that filled the air.

Owen excitedly showed his father his pile of bread, explaining the island's tradition of twice-daily bread delivery. His pride at recently being awarded the responsibility of the delivery was evident in his shining face as he told Ford about his favorite customers—those who gave him food or cash tips, of course. Ford laughed at that, meeting Katie's eyes above their son's head. "A born entrepreneur, this one."

"Either that or a born swindler," Katie teased, giving Owen a one-armed hug. "Meet you at the beach later, kiddo," she said as he fastened the cloth bags of bread loosely and packed them into the basket he carried.

"Gotcha, Mom." Owen waved, the bell jangling behind him.

"Busy morning for you, huh?" Katie wiped a smudge from Ford's cheek with a thumb, letting her hand linger a moment. She inhaled deeply, smiling that he did, indeed, smell just as she'd expected.

Ford inclined his head, scrubbing a hand across his face. "Busy enough. Best one of the day was on the helo. The patient's wife poked Phil and said, 'Can't you get us there faster—but not too high. Or too fast.'" He chuckled, remembering the first run of the morning.

Katie laughed with him, "I can totally understand that. Hurry but don't let me see what you gotta do to hurry."

"Daddy, want a donut hole?" Miri's gloved and glaze-covered hand popped up between them.

Ford reacted quickly, stepping back just enough to avoid wearing said glaze. "Did you make that, Miribelle?" With two fingers, he gingerly took the treat. Tossing it into his mouth, he affected a growl of appreciation. "Nothing like a sugar bomb after a busy morning, thanks." He winked at both girls, his eyebrows wiggling, sending them both into giggles.

Stripping off their gloves, Miri and Rory tandem carried the tray to the front of the bakery.

"That's two outta three plus the bonus kid. Where's Biscuit?"

Katie washed and dried her hands at the sink, dampening one end of a towel and handing it to him so he could do the same. "She's up front, coloring the windows last I saw. Reggie brought some window markers that made her day."

Ford stepped close and kept walking until he'd backed his wife up against the walk-in cooler. One hand resting on the door at each side of her, he let his body lean into her from shoulder to hip. Dipping his head, he nibbled along her favorite spot. He growled softly. "Ten years of being gone more than I'm home, and suddenly I can't think straight when I'm away from you." His breath tickled her ear.

She leaned forward and kissed him, his lips tasting of doughnut glaze. "I have noticed I keep looking for you around every corner. We got it bad, huh?"

"I hope so." He deepened the kiss as the two girls rounded the counters to wash their hands.

"Mommy, we're going to help Jill now." Seeing them, Miri rolled her eyes. "Oh, Daddy, for heaven's sake."

At Rory's giggle, Miri added, "See, Rory? I told you yours aren't the only ones that do that stuff."

At that, Ford threw back his head and laughed, rounding on the little girls. He bent low and stalked towards them, growling. "I might kiss my wife, but when it comes to meddling little girls? I'm a tickle monsterrr!" Spinning, he rose and dropped a quick kiss to Katie's cheek, then growled louder and chased them out the back door.

"Catch up at the beach later, Miri!" Katie dashed to the door to call out.

Ford stopped at the street's edge and turned, still laughing at the shrieking little girls running across the park. Arms spread, hands in the air, he said, "Exactly what time is 'later'?" He drew air quotes on the last word.

"Lunch-ish, when they meet the homeschool co-op at The Painted Parrot. After they eat, some of them are going to the kitchen with Matteo while others go to the boat with Nash," Katie said, leaning against the doorway. He looked so good, so strong and healthy. Her fingers tingled to touch him.

The email pictures of him immediately after the incident had been surfacing in her mind at random—his body twisted in pain, covered in blood and dirt, tubes snaking everywhere—making her belly clench and her hands shake. Right now, she grinned back at him, knowing what was coming next.

"Ish. Ish again? That does not answer the 'what time' question." Ford rolled his eyes, dramatically pointing to his watch.

"You're still wearing that thing? C'mon, man, acclimate!" Luke's truck slowed in the street, the sheriff leaning out his window.

Katie pointed at Ford and laughed, "You tell him, Sheriff!" Leaving them to it, she turned back into the bakery just in time for the oven timer to beep.

"Time to make the doughnuts," she murmured, grinning. That one, however lame, was never going to get old.

CHAPTER THIRTY-SEVEN

"YO HO, ME HEARTIES!" Nash swung Rory around and dropped her on the deck of the pontoon boat, her giggles sending her tumbling over into Miri.

"Little girls are definitely made of giggles," Nash declared, plopping Scarlett on top of the other two.

"And glitter!" Miri giggled.

"And bubble gum—they all like bubble gum." Owen rolled his eyes at his sisters and his friend.

"Where's the rum?" Scarlett piped up, sending all the adults into surprised laughter.

"Worry not, little one, we've got your vice right here." Jill held out a juice box.

As he stepped aboard the boat, Ford passed the juice box to his littlest daughter, tousling her hair on his way past her to the driver's seat.

"Captain Ford, I presume?" Katie teased as he took up a spot next to Nash at the boat's controls.

"Only captain on this boat is me, the rest are merely crew," Gabe called out from the dock where he freed the boat from its moorings and jumped aboard.

"I can captain, too! I can drive this thing!" Rory yelled from the back of the boat where she and Miri had already spread out a huge beach towel.

Owen looked at Gabe, the man's proud smile and confirming nod bringing an even bigger grin to Rory's face.

"You gotta teach me fast, Nash," Owen scowled, as a boy surrounded by girls and babies might do when faced with what he considered a test of his manhood. Hopping from one foot to the other, Owen hung over his father's shoulder, looking at the various gauges and buttons on the panel.

Clapping a hand to the top of the boy's head to avoid being slammed under the chin, Nash pushed Owen into the seat next to Ford. "Watch. Learn."

While Nash talked Ford and Owen through the basics of driving the pontoon boat, big hats, sunglasses and sunscreen were pulled from various places as Charlie settled on the bench seat with Katie.

Clad in a tiny orange life jacket, Zane wobbled from knee to knee and back to his mother where she sat on the deck floor.

Slathering the baby's visible skin with sunscreen, Jill thought this might just be the very definition of paradise—family, friends, sunshine and the sea. She smooched the baby's cheeks and squeezed him until he protested. Setting him back on his feet, he immediately crawled away to pull up and wobble about the legs of his father, who scooped him up into his arms.

From behind her blue floppy hat and sunglasses, Charlie watched her husband watch his daughter.

Leaning against the railing with his arms crossed, his shades pushed up, Gabe's head was tilted a bit as he listened to Nash instruct Owen on how to get the boat out of the slip and under way on the water, but his eyes were on Rory, a slight smile on his face. He never tired of watching her, of being amazed at her energy and brilliance. Finding and falling in love with Charlie—a grieving widow at the time—plus suddenly learning he was the father of a motherless nine year old girl had thrown him for a loop, but despite the challenges, they'd all found their way. Rory blossomed, Charlie thrived, and him? He adored them both with all of his heart.

From her spot, Katie thought she just might burst with contentment. She hadn't been able to breathe this easily for as long as she could remember—maybe before her mother had died, but her mother had been sick for so long that Katie could hardly remember ever feeling secure, safe and happy. Until now. The realization that had first occurred to her in the hospital garden with Ford bloomed fully under the sunshine and salty air as the wind tangled her ponytail and her family and friends laughed around her. While Ford had hurt her deeply when he'd shut her out after the incident, she'd come to understand that he'd believed with all of his being that he was doing it for her. Just like her secret that was meant to be a gift, but when it all went to hell she'd wanted only to protect him from the self blame she'd known he'd feel. Toying with her shooting star pendant, Katie watched Ford ease out of the captain's chair to let Owen fully enjoy steering the boat out into the open water himself. Under Nash's expert guidance, the boy was truly captain for the moment.

Catching Ford's eye, Katie smiled and shifted in her seat, making room for him. He slid onto the seat with a barely suppressed wince that brought his wife's eyes to his face.

"You're hurting," she said, reaching out to cup his face, stroking his right temple with her thumb.

Ford shrugged. "The usual."

Katie rolled her eyes. "The usual doesn't bring this." Her fingers rubbed across the furrows in his forehead.

"Or this." She brushed the tight lines next to his eye.

Ford closed his eyes, her touch soothing him in a way no meds or booze ever could.

"Still, not bad," Ford assured her, putting an arm around her and settling back into the seat, pulling her against him.

"Any thoughts about a plan for Amos, Katie?" Jill asked, deftly saving a wayward seashell from her son's mouth.

Katie shook her head. "Talbot wants him to stay in the hospital for a few more days, get his heart medication regulated and all. That buys me a bit of time to work something out."

"It's so hard when someone so independent can't be left alone anymore," Charlie said.

"Especially when he thinks he's doing just fine, thank you very much," Gabe put in. He loved the old man like a grandfather, having spent many hours together. It was Amos who'd convinced him to do more than just renovate the property, to upgrade the cottages and offer a more private, luxury experience for families. The old man wanted Gabe's property venture to succeed, to keep both Gabe's and Nash's family here, to keep the place a largely private yet thriving island.

"My biggest obstacle is I don't want to take him from his home at this point. All of you know how talks about Bessie as if she's right there with him at home. He never mentions her away from his place." Katie sighed.

"Hey look, an army man!" Rory called from her seat at the boat's fishing stern.

They all looked ashore in the direction Rory was pointing.

"I didn't see him," Jill said from the middle of the boat where she'd stood up when Rory'd called out.

"Me, either." Charlie looked to Gabe.

"I did and he had a b-big gun," Miri said from her spot between her father's knees where she'd flown when Rory had pointed. Wide-eyed, she burrowed into his chest, clutching his shirt with both hands. Ford held her close, his eyes scanning the shore.

Owen spoke up, "I saw his back going into the woods just as Rory yelled."

The three men exchanged glances that did not go missed by their wives.

Charlie slid to the deck floor with a smile for the baby, gathering him to her and motioning for Scarlett to come sit on her lap. She busied them with the colorful blocks they'd been playing with, keeping them out of view of anyone off the boat.

Ford hugged Miri close, his eyes still on the shore. "Tell me what you saw, baby."

Rory joined her friend, slipping her hand into Miri's. "It's okay, Miri, tell your daddy. Our daddies and Uncle Nash will take care of us."

Miri nodded. "It was an army man like you, Daddy. With a really big g-gun. And H-halloween painted on his face."

Her heart pounding in her ears, Katie followed Charlie's example and slid to the deck floor, drawing Miri and Rory with her. Miri let go of Ford and crawled into her mother's lap, her eyes wide, breath fast and frightened.

"It's okay, baby, you're okay," Katie murmured, rubbing her daughter's back in rhythmic circles.

Ford leaned in and kissed the little girl's forehead, his gaze meeting Katie's for a beat.

Moving to the railing next to Gabe, he spoke quietly. "I can man the boat, you're both familiar with the area."

Gabe shook his head. "On the off chance it goes bad, your skills are better suited. Plus I can get them back to safety faster being captain and all." The last was said with a wink as he moved to the captain's chair where Owen sat wide-eyed, watching and listening. "Scoot over, Cap, let me show you how it's done." Gabe said, his big hand squeezing Owen's shoulder.

Nash opened the compartment below the rail next to the control panel. His back to everyone, he slid his gun into his pocket, followed by ammo. "You armed?" he asked Ford quietly, giving a grunt of appreciation at the other man's short nod.

As Gabe brought the boat in close to the shore, Nash and Ford hopped off into the shallow water and headed for the tree line where the girls had pointed. Gabe had the boat out of the bay and on the open sea before the other two men's feet had hardly hit the water.

"Is Daddy doing war again, Mommy?" Miri's grip bit into Katie's arms.

Owen whipped his head around to his sister. "No, Miri!" At her startled expression, he gentled his voice, "Dad and Nash are just checking things out. Let's play jacks, okay?" The boy pulled the game pieces from multiple cargo pockets.

Katie smiled at her son, who grinned and ducked his head, busying his sister and Rory—and himself—with the game.

Checking his phone and walkie-talkie, Gabe laid both on the console within reach and turned the boat to head home. He'd come back for the men after this crew was home safely with Luke and his deputies on alert. As the boat sped across the open sea, Charlie moved to sit on his knee, the littlest ones playing happily between Jill and Katie's legs.

"Does this happen often?" Katie asked, holding her hands out for Scarlett and Zane to fill them with the blocks.

Charlie shook her head. "Not this level of alarm, no. Luke and the guys usually just check out any drifters and hermits on these outlying islands, and life goes on. Some move on, others stay a long time, living on their own. We've not had any major trouble since I've been here."

Gabe popped the top on the bottle of lemonade Jill handed him from the cooler, one hand on the steering wheel. "Since I came out here after 9/11, we've had only three issues with drifters that involved arrests."

Katie relaxed a bit at his words, feeling more concerned than afraid. She rocked slightly, Scarlett in her arms. She couldn't bear to think that Ford would survive all that he had only to meet a violent drifter out here in paradise. The irony was laughable, even amid her fear.

"I vote we eat," Charlie declared, opening the basket next to her feet.

"I'm starved!" Owen clutched his stomach dramatically.

Katie kicked him lightly. "You're always starved, kid."

"Hear, hear." Gabe grabbed the boy in a headlock, still keeping one hand on the dash as the boat moved steadily on the sea. "Starving boys make strong men."

Jill laughed, "Starving boys make starving men, more like."

With everyone distracted eating and playing on the boat deck floor, Charlie leaned into Gabe, her voice for his ears only. "You don't think—"

Gabe cut her off with a shake of his head. "I don't." He softened the sting of his terse words with a one-armed hug and a kiss pressed to her temple.

CHAPTER THIRTY-EIGHT

"TWO ARMED DRIFTERS in less than a week," Nash commented, sliding onto a bar stool in front of Gabe.

Gabe looked across the room filled with the evening crowd while he mixed a drink and set it in front of a couple more interested in each other than him. With a grin at them, he moved back down the bar and leaned in closer to Nash. "Amos's place and that little island aren't that far apart, across the water."

"You think it's the same one?" Nash considered the idea for a moment.

"Ford's the one who's seen both stash sites, let's see if anything makes him tingle." Gabe tipped his head towards the other man walking around the corner into the bar from the restaurant side.

"I'm not talking about my tingles with you two." Eyebrow raised, Ford slid onto the bar stool next to Nash.

Gabe rolled his eyes as Nash hooted out loud.

Ford dropped his voice, tapping a finger on the bar. "At both sites, same provisions. Look at the pictures."

Gabe nodded. "I noticed that."

"Me too." Nash scrolled to the pictures on his phone to get another look.

"I sent the pictures and locations to Luke, filled him in. He's going to look for himself tomorrow," Gabe said.

"You said this level of concern doesn't happen often," Ford commented, finishing the glass of water Gabe had set in front of him.

Nash shook his head. "I can count on one hand the number of times I've been this bothered by a drifter in all the years we've been here."

"Less than that, probably," Gabe agreed, moving back down the bar to chat with new arrivals.

"Hey, Nash, Matteo has outdone himself again. Dude needs a raise," Jane called out as she came around the restaurant's corner for her shift in the bar.

"The hell he does," Nash countered. "Diva already costs me more than most of you combined."

The chef, well worth every penny, was a native to the islands who made every bite of even the most basic menu a delight. The man in question strolled into the bar a few paces behind Jane. "Perfection has its price." Matteo's devilish grin was infectious.

"Perfection my ass," Nash laughed. "I could do it—if I ever bothered to cook."

Matteo took the ribbing in stride, his jovial nature a big part of his success with the restaurant—plus the fact that he truly loved food and was ridiculously talented behind the stove.

The Painted Parrot had started out as just a bar, one that had been salvaged by Gabe and Nash after it was ravaged by Hurricane Yasi. Its owners, Bill and Marjorie, had decided to sell and move closer to family. When Gabe and Nash had partnered to buy the place, they'd begun by reconstructing the cottages and the bar themselves with a little local help. The idea to add a full scale restaurant came about when they'd found Matteo at a bar in the nearest all-inclusive resort one night. Desperate to escape bar tending and try his skills in a kitchen, Matteo had convinced them to gamble on him and had come to work for them when the only kitchen was the small one behind the bar where Nash now stood.

"What's up, Wonderchef?" Nash gestured to an empty seat next to him.

"I'm on, so just a quick moment." Matteo leaned against the bar and glanced around. "It's probably no big deal, but after that shark bait investigator last year, it made me twitchy."

Gabe stopped in his tracks and turned around. "What made you twitchy?"

"Twice now I've had a take-out order from a man I've never seen before—ordering Amos's exact usual." Matteo rubbed his chin thoughtfully. "I mean even down to the number of butter pats and the way he likes his sweet tea. At first I didn't notice it wasn't one of you, as one of my part timers took the order. Jane took the second one and brought it to my attention, but the man had already gone."

Ford's eyebrows shot up and he pushed away from the bar. "I need eyes on Amos and my family."

Giving Gabe a nod that he'd have eyes on Charlie and Rory as well as his own family in minutes, Nash matched Ford's stride out of the bar.

Matteo watched them go and turned back to Gabe. "It just didn't make sense that it was none of you getting Amos's order as usual."

"Thanks for the heads up. If he comes back, signal me before he leaves if you can." Gabe took out his phone.

"Hey, Luke?"

With a nod, Matteo returned to his kitchen while Gabe finished the call and returned to his customers, not alarmed but uneasy at the strange goings on.

CHAPTER THIRTY-NINE

WITH AN HOUR TO SPARE before the bakery opened, Katie left Reggie finishing up and took her coffee to the sea's edge. The peacefulness of the sky just before sunrise was matched only by the twilight just after sunset. She walked to The Painted Parrot and sat at one of the tables, the bar dark in the blue dawn's light.

Propping her feet on a chair, Katie looked about at the big brass hurricane lantern that was lit on special days or when someone was missing at sea, the decorative maritime signal flags of various colors fluttering in the breeze. Amos loved it here. He'd been a fixture on his barstool or out here at this very table for a long time, she'd been told. When he'd become unable to get himself here daily, the old island man only allowed Gabe to fetch him three or four times a week, refusing to be a burden. Since Katie and the kids had found him and moved to the island, he'd been persuaded more often, yet still insisted on spending much of his days alone on his fishing dock. He was fond of saying that's where his lady love—his wife of sixty years, now gone nearly five years—lingered, at their home, on their porch, beside him at the dock.

How could she part him from that by bringing him to the cottage with her to care for him? Yet how could she wrangle three kids and her bakery from Amos's tiny home on the cove? Amid all of this, her accidental secret burned inside her chest. She couldn't live with it, yet she also couldn't tell Ford. At a loss about it all, Katie gazed out to the sea, the deep, velvety blue twilight ebbing into the periwinkle and orange of the sunrise. Despite the challenges, maybe because of them in some way, she felt more alive than she had in a long time— or was that Ford's doing?—and smiled. This life thing they were caught up in sure wasn't easy, but nothing worthwhile ever was. Katie stood and stretched her arms to the sky, bringing them down into a sun salutation yoga series just as the waves burst into glittering gems with the sun's first rays over the horizon.

*   *   *

Running up the beach, Ford slowed to watch his wife move fluidly through the yoga poses, the morning sun igniting fleeting copper streaks in her dark brown hair, her tank top clinging to her curves. That right there was a sight he'd never, ever tire of. He'd been turning the problem of caring for Amos over and over in his mind, letting it toss about, hoping some idea would shake loose, but watching Katie's silhouette against the sunlight cleared everything else from his mind. Ford couldn't believe she'd never thought herself worthy of being put first. He'd failed bigtime if she'd thought all this time he was just along for the ride between deployments because he'd been determined to do the right thing when she'd gotten pregnant ten years ago. He'd thought he'd cherished her better than that. It made no sense, yet he knew the insecurities and painful lessons from childhood often didn't make much sense. The heart dealt with deep hurt however it could to survive.

He'd always wanted to make life easier for her, to see her smile, to know she was taken care of. In this moment, he realized that in the years of near constant deployments, she'd built the life he'd wanted to build with her—mostly without him. And she'd done it apparently believing she and their children classified as a longterm fix-it project for him. Ford sighed deeply, regret burning a hole in his stomach. After all he'd been through, after all he'd learned, he was more than ready to live simply—all he wanted or needed was this woman and the life they shared. While it seemed she was on board with that, too, he needed her to feel cherished, to understand he was here because of *her*—not just because of Owen or Miri or Scarlett.

*   *   *

She felt his presence before he'd even reached her side, the little hairs on her arm prickling in awareness, her body warming in remembrance of waking next to him this morning. She'd lain still, barely breathing, for watching him sleep was a rarity since his latest return. He'd opened his eyes and, with a nuzzle to her neck, moved to cover her body with his. Making love in the dim quiet of the predawn had brought tears to her eyes, tears he'd kissed away without question, wrapping her in his arms and holding on.

"Fancy meeting you here." Ford dropped to the sand beside her now, his t-shirt hanging off one shoulder, his breath still fast from his run.

Katie smiled, running a hand over his stubbled jaw. "Good run?"

He nodded, tweaking her ponytail with one hand. "Decent going until I was distracted by a sun goddess."

"Ppfftt," Katie blew a raspberry at him. She didn't take compliments graciously, they made her squirm.

Ford laughed, letting her hair go, his hands dropping to hang between his knees.

They both gazed out to the sea as boats came and went, the island's vendors waiting on the shore.

"Hey!" Gabe waved as he steered the JohnBToo ashore, Nash hopping to the sand to tie them off.

Waving back, Katie sighed. "I don't know what to do about Amos."

"Me either," Ford admitted.

"Home is so important to him, or I'd just move him in," she said.

"I know. He talks often about seeing Bessie Jo every day, in the house, on the porch, next to him on the dock," Ford replied.

Katie drew circles in the sand in front of her crossed legs. "He does that more and more lately, it seems."

Glancing at his watch, Ford stood and held out a hand, tugging Katie up to stand.

Hand in hand, they walked across the park in silence, sharing a wordless, lingering parting kiss on the sidewalk as Ford went inside the house to shower and Katie stepped into the bakery, already bustling with morning customers.

Nothing had to be solved at this moment except Mrs. Harlow's need for her morning pastries and the kids next door's need for breakfast. Katie had to admit it was nice knowing Ford was at home, helping the kids get moving this morning instead of her running back and forth from the house to the bakery. They'd all join her shortly for breakfast before scattering for the day.

She smiled at Mrs. Harlow. "I tried a twist on your favorite lemon orange scone this morning, and I'd love your opinion."

CHAPTER FORTY

"KATIE? KIDS?" Ford stepped into the house, not expecting anyone to be home in the late afternoon of a sunny island day. He'd stopped by midshift to look for his heavy duty flashlight, as the one Luke had issued him was a joke, in his opinion. The house was dim and quiet, the only sounds made by appliances humming and the startled lizard thrashing about from the cage in Owen's room. Ford still didn't know if that thing was male or female.

Striding across the living room, he opened a side table drawer and lifted out the flashlight he'd forgotten when he moved out in a hurry—he'd needed it twice already this morning. He pushed the drawer closed with his knee, checking the flashlight's battery with a quick flick of the switch. Satisfied it was ready, he snapped it into a loop on his utility belt and turned to go, his eye catching a piece of paper fluttering to the floor. Intending to stick it back in the drawer it had fallen from, he picked up the paper and glanced at it as he reopened the drawer. He tilted his head, trying to process the words he'd just read. Sinking to the chair, he blinked twice, shaking his head a little as if it would help him understand what he held in his hand. His headache ramped up, thrumming along with his increasing pulse. Crumpling the paper in his fist, Ford shoved to his feet and strode out the door in search of his wife—and an explanation for these impossible words he held crushed in his hand.

* * *

On the beach, Katie tied orange tape to a wooden stake, listening to Reggie tell the kids about the loggerhead turtle nest they had just marked off to protect it from being trampled. As most of Reggie's groups, this group was made up of both island kids and tourist kids, all eager to finish marking the nests—as this was number six, the novelty was wearing off—and race down to the Snack Shack for ice cream. A sleeping Zane against her shoulder, Jill nudged Katie's leg with her foot. When Katie looked at her questioningly, she jerked her head behind Katie. Katie looked around to see Ford standing a few feet away, his stance rigid, his face impassive. His eyes were hidden behind his aviators, but it was clear there was something very wrong.

"Hi, Daddy!" Miri ran to his side to hug his legs.

Ford reached an arm down to return his daughter's hug but didn't swing her up into his arms. "A quick word with Mommy, okay?" He forced a smile at the girl who beamed back at him and ran back to her friends.

Katie heard the terseness in his voice, saw his fisted hands, and went to him immediately.

"What's happened?" she asked, automatically placing a hand on his arm. She almost backed up a step at the coiled tension in him, his arm hard as steel under her hand.

"Walk," Ford ordered, turning to walk away from the group of kids.

Worried, Katie followed him for a few minutes before she spoke again. "Ford, what's going on?"

Glancing to ensure the kids were far enough away, Ford held out a crumpled piece of paper.

Wordlessly, Katie's eyes widened in horror as she realized what he held.

"Ford—"

"What in goddamned hell is this?" He thrust the paper at her, pushing his shades up. His eyes blazed hot enough that Katie fully expected to be incinerated on the spot.

Licking her suddenly dry lips, Katie took the paper and pocketed it. She didn't need to read it again.

"Let's go talk."

"Now," Ford demanded, his bulk solid and unmoving against her hand.

Katie took a deep breath, looking down at her bare feet in the sand. "I intended to tell you—"

"What is it about?" Ford snarled, giving each word a separate weight, shoving his shaking hands into his pockets as he struggled for control.

Katie could quote the short, poignant note from a dear friend who'd lived near them in Kansas.

The note that had offered her friend's heartfelt condolences on Katie's loss.

The loss of Katie's micro preemie baby boy. The baby she'd intended to surprise Ford with but had never had the chance.

The note that was dated barely eight months ago.

Knowing she owed him so much more than an explanation, but unable to come up with the right words, Katie's hands covered her mouth. Dragging in a deep breath, she tried again, "Right after you deployed, I found out I was pregnant."

Stunned, Ford's knees gave out and he sat down, hard. Katie joined him, reaching out to take his hands in hers, only to have him hold them up, away from her. That hurt almost as much as what she was about to say.

"You didn't tell me about a baby. A *lost* baby." Ford's voice was tight, his hands still in the air. He didn't want to be touched by her right now.

"I wanted to surprise you when you came home on leave—I would have been six months along and thought it would be fun to see your face when you found out." Wiping away tears that trickled down her face, Katie gazed out to the sea. "Everything happened so fast, Ford. I went into early labor one morning at only twenty-two weeks. I checked into the hospital so they could try and stop it and—" she paused to take a deep, shuddering breath. "While I was there literally fighting to keep our baby from being born too soon, you were being blown to bits on the other side of the world."

Ford closed his eyes tightly against the punch of pain—pain from the tsunami of sudden grief, from his mounting headache, from his heart breaking. He wrapped his arms around his knees and rocked. It didn't work. Shoving to his feet, he whirled around, eyes blazing steel blue. "I lost a son eight fucking months ago, and I find out his existence by accidentally picking up a piece of goddamned paper?"

Katie jumped to her feet as well. "I'm so sorry, Ford. It-it all happened so fast and then you refused to see me. I shut down."

Through the haze of his fury, Ford could almost see his part in the fiasco, but the grief and anger were far too much. Blinding colors flashing through his head, sounds breaking apart, crashing into random, deafening noise, Ford stumbled as he turned and ran down the beach. He unbuckled his utility belt and let it fall as he ran, ditching the weight and the radio. His phone hit the sand shortly after.

Katie watched him go, her hands pressed tightly to her mouth, tears flowing down her cheeks. She knew that now, after all they'd been through, she'd truly lost him.

CHAPTER FORTY-ONE

FORD RAN THROUGH his blinding fury, down the beach and up into the mountains. Hours passed while he lay prone in the sand, his arm over his eyes while the damn migraine beat the hell out of his skull. Once he could stand, he wandered aimlessly before he looped back around and found himself at The Painted Parrot with minutes to go before closing. This time of night the lights were just a little dimmer, fostering more of a mood for romance and winding down for the night. A few couples danced or ate a late meal at the tables; the bar itself stood empty except for Nash behind it.

Nash set a glass filled with ice and a pitcher of water on the bar, waiting while Ford approached.

He met Ford's stricken gaze. "Good to see you, Ace. You had one more hour before we sent out the cavalry."

The other man's face was etched in stark relief, his eyes bloodshot, shirt soaked in sweat. He rubbed a hand up and down his face, scrubbing at his eyes before draining the first glass and refilling it. His voice was ragged. "Thanks. Bourbon?"

Nash expertly concealed his surprise as he turned to the shelf behind him, this being the first time he'd known Ford to ask for more than one beer. Not that he blamed the man at all after what he'd heard Ford had been through today—or even before. He poured the liquor into a stocky glass, watched Ford down it with a hiss and tap the glass on the bar for more.

"Again and put three more right there."

Nash frowned but complied, watching Ford contemplate the glasses. He breathed a sigh of relief when Ford tossed back the contents of the first, then the second and third glasses, setting them upside down on the bar without asking for more.

"Rough night, I hear." Nash tossed the words over his shoulder as he replaced the amber bottle high on the shelf. His personal indulgent vice of choice, the bourbon was an import purchased from one of the resorts on a bigger island—expensive and rarely asked for at The Painted Parrot. Ford, elbows on the bar, head resting in his hands, didn't reply.

Nash squeezed Ford's shoulder as he walked by, taking a few minutes to stroll through the bar. He ushered the last couple out of the bar with good wishes and a shake of his head, laughing at their tipsy honeymoon silliness. Nash rolled down the rattan shades that kept most nocturnal critters out of the bar and turned back to where Ford sat. He went around the bar and pulled a beer from the cooler and, without commentary, leaned back against the counter behind the bar and sipped, waiting.

Ford stirred the ice in his glass around with a finger, the fingers of the other hand clenched in his hair. Belting back several shots of good bourbon had blurred the sharpest edges of his headache and his anger, but it didn't seem to touch his grief, making him a somber man. As a rule, he didn't drink anymore after he'd spent three weeks in a bourbon-soaked oblivion during his recovery. While it efficiently obliterated his problems, it also obliterated his life. Tonight, he'd needed to dull the raging grief and anger before he did something more stupid than get blind drunk.

"I left her a few days ago." Ford's voice was rough yet quiet. Reaching in his shirt pocket, he dangled the B&B key from his fingertips, letting it fall to the bar top with a clatter. "But that pales in comparison to the secret she kept from me."

Ford continued to stir the ice. "Since I've been here, she's pushed me out the door every day. Go, Ford, I don't want you here. Every. Day. All this time she's been treating my mistakes as unforgivable when she—she never told me about a *lost baby.*" His grief crescendoed, fueling his anger; Ford stood and spun, sending the water glass hurtling against a table where it shattered.

Nash winced, but stood where he was. Powerful grief deserved powerful reaction.

Gabe appeared in the doorway, pausing to survey the glass. He looked at Nash, then Ford. As a father who'd been kept from his child for nine years, he understood the sharp sting of time gone forever.

"I need air." Ford pushed off the barstool, with a slight falter before he found his feet.

Nash glanced about the place one last time, then flipped the music and lights off. Rounding the bar, he followed Gabe and Ford out onto the beach where Ford's legs gave out and he sat down hard at the edge of the water. The two men sat on either side of him. He was pretty hammered, coupled with exhaustion; lights out would likely be coming soon.

"We reconnected, y'know?" Ford's emphasis on the world reconnected left no doubt as to what he meant.

"Then—" He swallowed hard, rubbing a hand over his chest. "Then I overheard her saying the sight of me hurts her. So I left. And now this."

Nash shifted, letting his shoulder press against Ford's. "Ouch."

Minutes passed, and Ford grew still and quiet.

Gabe toyed with shells in the sand. "We better get you to a bed, Ace. I'm not hauling your dead-weight carcass off this beach."

Ford didn't answer, letting them tug him to his feet.

"Let's crash him on my couch. No need to dump him on Katie," Nash said.

Gabe grunted as Ford leaned into him heavily. "He's in for an ugly day."

"Yeah. I figure we'll drag him out on the boat with us—get him going." Nash grinned.

"You know I can hear you, right? And I will kick your asses if I wake up on a boat," Ford grumbled, his head down, watching his feet.

Gabe shook his head as they tugged Ford up the steps of Nash and Jill's cottage, the lamps in the windows casting a warm glow.

The door opened, and Jill appeared. "What happened?" She moved aside to let them in.

"Bourbon happened. He's about to be a lead weight," Nash said, shoving Ford onto the couch where he promptly tumbled over. Ford mumbled a few words and went quiet.

"See you at the boat." Gabe clapped Nash's shoulder on his way out the door.

Jill shook out a blanket over Ford while Nash pushed off the man's shoes.

Looking down at his friend, Nash sighed, enveloping his wife in a hug and pressing a kiss to her head.

"Did you know?" he asked quietly.

Jill shook her head. "I suspected something was bothering her but no, I didn't know until he showed up on the beach. After the shouting match, Charlie and I were with her until she insisted she wanted to be alone. Do I need to go to her?"

"Maybe text and let her know he's safe."

"I can't imagine what they're going through." Jill reached down to smooth the blanket over Ford's shoulder. "Katie seems certain the damage is too great for them to make it."

"It's one thing to do battle yourself, another thing to try and show someone else they can do it." Nash reached out for his wife's hand. "We know that all too well."

As the night deepened and the breeze riffled the curtains throughout the house, an owl hooted outside. Nash's arm was snug around his wife as he drifted off, the baby sighing softly from his connecting bed. All of these things soothed Jill, yet she remained wide awake, worrying for her friend and the man on her couch.

*   *   *

After insisting that Charlie and Jill go home, Katie had done the bedtime routine with the kids on autopilot and settled in the hammock in a daze. She desperately wanted to go to Ford. Despite all that stood between them, she knew she was the only person in the world who could truly share his grief over the baby. It sucked going through that alone, she knew this. But, from Jill's text, she knew Ford had been falling-down drunk tonight and would be passed out cold for a while yet. She sighed deeply, pulling the lightweight blanket around her tightly and setting the hammock to swinging with a push of her bare foot hanging over the side. From her angle in the hammock, she could see part of the sky, the stars bright and bold against the deep indigo night. She had no idea what constellations she was looking at—that was Ford's realm. His and Amos's. The two men had been spending hours laying out under the stars with the kids, telling them stories and pointing out constellations. It was that love of the stars that had led her to name the baby Orion. Her hand clutching the silver shooting star pendant at her throat, remembering how tiny he'd been, she drifted off to sleep, tear tracks shining silver in the starlight.

CHAPTER FORTY-TWO

"YOU'D THINK NEITHER ONE of you assholes has ever had a hangover before," Ford grumbled, albeit quietly as to not encourage the merciless marching band stomping and shrieking about in his head.

"On the contrary, my friend, we know coddling the damn thing doesn't happen with a kingdom to run." Gabe's laugh was jarring.

Ford held his head in his hands in hopes of keeping it from flying off into the wide blue yonder, his groan louder as fresh pain stabbed behind his eyes. "I swear these shades are useless," he muttered, sitting back against the bar, clapping a hand over his eyes.

"Give us some credit, we considered taking you out on the boat, but mercy prevailed," Nash said as Matteo came around the corner from the kitchen and set plates of eggs, toast and bacon in front of them with a clatter that rang Ford's bells anew.

"Mother of God," Ford muttered, hand to his eyes, reaching blindly for his cup of coffee. Given the first cup and four pills when Nash had pushed him into the shower first thing this morning, it'd been refilled repeatedly since. Helpfully, Gabe slid the elusive cup closer to his hand.

"Lukewarm, drink it down," Gabe said, setting a fresh, steaming cup next to that one.

Nash sat next to Ford, eyeing Gabe over his own cup.

Ford ate methodically. He started to speak a few times, but changed his mind and continued to eat.

Gabe stood behind the bar, sipping in silence as the dawn fully broke and the sun rose in the sky. He leaned forward to look out at the sea, glittering in the morning sun. His hum of appreciation was echoed by Nash.

Ford's radio squawked to life just as he thought he might be able to open his eyes all the way. He fumbled for it with a curse, turning the volume down to what he considered a more humane level.

"Need to call off shift?" Nash asked.

Ford shook his head and stood, stretching for the ceiling with a groan and audible pops from his body.

Leaving the shades in place, he looked from Nash to Gabe as the radio squawked again. "Thanks."

Both men raised their cups in salute, watching Ford walk away, breaking into a halting jog once outside.

"Well, that went well," Nash remarked. "He's up and functioning."

"You call Luke?"

Gabe nodded. "Didn't see any reason we couldn't maybe bring Katie a little peace of mind by having eyes on him today."

Nash grunted an agreement, sliding a case of clean glasses under the counter.

The two men readied the bar for the day, moving in an easy rhythm born from years of working side by side.

On the other side of the wall, the restaurant came alive, the smells of food cooking and the sounds of kitchen activity and early risers in search of breakfast joining the full brightness of the morning sun to fill Gabe's senses. He loved this island life he'd created after years of noise and fire, trauma and tragedy in the city. While he'd thrived in his life as a firefighter, it had been time to move on. This life was a return to home of sorts for him, the son of a fisherman who had grown up along the coast of Rhode Island. Different coast, different climate, same peace. He could only hope that this life could bring Ford even a little of that peace.

"Tough stuff to watch, much less go through," Nash commented, scooping the breakfast dishes into a tub to return to the kitchen. "You think they'll be okay?"

Gabe shrugged, wiping down the bar. "It's not the same thing, but I'm not sure I can ever forgive Lilith—even in death—for keeping Rory from me all those years. I'd like to say love conquers all, but secrets, anger and grief are powerful forces."

The two men finished in silence and, with the bar ready to go several hours before opening, they glanced at one another and headed for the JohnBToo. The open sea under impossibly blue skies beckoned them, the waves dotted with red and yellow sails, dolphins splashing off in the distance, the sun glinting like diamonds on the water droplets they kicked up. Nothing couldn't be made better by time on the sea, under the sun—even if that time was spent unobtrusively searching for signs of a stranger.

CHAPTER FORTY-THREE

LEAVING THE GIRLS' ROOM where he'd read three-that-felt-like-fifteen bedtime stories and chuckled along with the endless giggles his daughters were full of, Ford was headed to return to the B&B for the night. Rubbing his temple, he was past ready to sleep off the massive caffeine crash he knew would be hitting soon. After beating the hangover into grumbling submission and working his shift, he'd spent the evening with the kids, Katie deliberately busy at the bakery. Before he took another step on his way out of the house, a muffled sob hit like an arrow to his heart.

He stopped at the doorway of the master bedroom. His wife stood in front of an open drawer, her head bowed. With one hand inside the drawer, the other one fisted against her mouth, another sob escaped.

"Katie..." He was at a complete loss for words. Anger still snapped and sizzled between them, but love born from countless hours in her arms, months of longing for her time and again, wouldn't let him pretend he hadn't heard her sobs.

She wiped her face and sighed deeply, not turning around.

"I'm so sorry, Ford." Her whisper was barely audible, but it was all he needed to cross the room to her side. He stood close, his body warming hers.

Katie leaned into him slightly. "I know you're angry, but I-I really need you to hear me out."

Looking into the drawer where her hand rested, Ford saw a small wooden box with a shooting star etched across the top. The dull throb in his chest became a sharp, stabbing pain. He rubbed his hand across it absently.

Katie's breath hitched on a sob when he reached inside the drawer and put his hand on hers. After a moment, he squeezed her hand gently and lifted the box from the drawer. He held in it both hands, his thumbs running across the shooting star and the name etched there, meeting her tear-filled eyes with tears in his own.

Katie moved to sit cross-legged in the middle of the bed. Joining her, Ford set the box on the bed between them, fingers stroking the textured design over and over.

He cleared his throat. "Tell me about him."

Katie drew the box closer to her, her fingers tightening on the top.

Caressing her cheek, his thumb wiping away a tear, Ford waited.

"Please." His voice barely above a whisper, he gently pushed aside her hand to open the box. She sat silently, more tears spilling over.

A tiny camouflage print infant gown lay folded on top. The words *Daddy's Littlest Soldier* were embroidered in blue across the impossibly small garment. Lifting the little gown from the box, Ford set it on his leg, his fingers caressing the words.

"Tell me," he said again.

Katie shook her head.

"In—" He swallowed, hard, and tried again. "In the span of seconds, I was both given a son and had him torn from me—I have nothing of him. His father should know and remember him, Katie."

She whimpered at that, lifting out a soft little knitted blue hat that easily fit into the center of her palm.

Ford took the hat from her, slipping it over three of his fingers.

"Impossibly small," he whispered, his thumb caressing the soft yarn.

"Too small," Katie said. "H-He never opened his eyes...they told me it was too soon. Little kitten eyes, they weren't ready."

Ford closed his eyes tightly, his hand closing over the hat.

"I've never wanted anything so badly in my life as I wanted to see his eyes." Katie lowered her face to her arms, wrapped tightly around drawn-up knees. With halting, barely audible words, she told her baby's father about the too-few hours their youngest son had lived.

Ford kept the tiny hat fisted in his hand, head bowed as he listened, the other hand curled around his wife's ankle.

When Katie's voice trailed off, they were silent for a few moments.

She met his eyes when he looked up, the pools of blue deep and sad. "I didn't mean to keep it—him—from you, Ford. It went from a surprise to a horror so fast. Add in that you nearly died then refused to see me, I—I just shut down."

Ford raised his hands then dropped them. His hand shook as he lifted four pictures from the box.

"Ford." She lay a hand over his.

He didn't look at her, tugging his hand free. "I need to see." The words felt like ground glass in his throat.

The first picture would have brought him to his knees had he not been sitting down. His breath whooshed out, hard, leaving him struggling for air. The camera was zoomed in close on the tiny boy lying on his mother's chest draped in a camo blanket trimmed in blue, the minuscule blue hat askew on his wee kiwi-sized head. Tracing the baby's image with a fingertip, a soft keening sound escaped him as he sucked in a ragged breath.

Katie didn't want to look at the pictures. She'd stopped taking them out every night, then every week. But she couldn't deny Ford, nor could she leave him to look at them alone.

The second picture was Orion clad in only a scrap of cotton, cupped in his mother's hands, his little legs sprawled, showing just how impossibly small he'd been.

"Unreal," Ford whispered.

The third, and last, picture was Ford's complete undoing. Pressing it to his heart, he sat motionless, his big body bent forward.

A nurse had taken a picture of Katie with the baby tucked against her chest. Her shirt open, the two of them were skin to skin, the baby draped with the camo blanket. Katie's hands cupped him protectively, dwarfing his tiny body, her eyes closed, tears falling on the little face.

"Holy Mother of God," Ford breathed. He thought he might suffocate from the pain. Despite all he'd been through, nothing had felt like this fire and ice consuming him inside and out.

Katie fought the powerful need to flee from his pain, from her pain. The need to check on the kids pulled at her, the bakery called to her, the moonlit beach whispered to her—everything and anything came together and fairly screamed for her attention. Amid it all, the need to comfort this man she loved so much won out. With a deep, bracing breath, she nudged Ford to turn his body and lie back on the bed, wrapping her arms around his shoulders as his arms came around her waist. She stroked his head where he rested against her.

For the first time since his birth, little Orion's parents grieved their loss together.

* * *

At some point, Katie fell into an exhausted sleep. While she slept deeply, curled into a tight ball against his side, Ford lay wide awake until he could be still no longer. Moving carefully, he stood and tugged the blanket over Katie, who murmured briefly before sinking deeper into sleep.

The opening of that little box, hearing the details about his tiny son the night before, had not only allowed the two of them to grieve together, it had also opened his eyes with shocking clarity.

They'd built their life together on trust, two world-weary, lonely kids throwing their lots in together. Without trust in one to care for the other during life's most horrific moments, what in God's name did they have?

The words he'd overheard Katie say to Jill rang in his head. Miri's cries when she worried for him echoed. The pictures of a child he hadn't even known existed before he was gone burned in his mind. Those words, those cries, that secret screamed louder than anything he'd ever heard.

Tying his shoes, Ford left the house quietly. Setting off at a run, his thoughts churned wildly as he tried to come up with what he should do next. How could he prove to Katie he'd be here for her—get her to remember that his track record had been good before hello, brain injury? He knew it sounded like an excuse, for he'd been well enough to change his decree that kept her away for a long time. He couldn't blame his injury when he'd been functional for awhile now. Not telling him about Orion was her way of defending herself against what she saw as further betrayal. What a mess. He hoped the run would help untangle things, help him see what to do next.

CHAPTER FORTY-FOUR

SPRAYING DOWN THE DECK of the JohnBToo before a midday charter, the sun blazing over the whitecapping waves, Gabe was stopped in his tracks when his phone went off with his wife's 911 alert at the same time as both Ford's and Nash's phones.

The men's eyes shot to one another's faces as they reached in pockets for the ringing phones. In synchronized motions, they all three leapt over the boat's side onto the sand and headed to The Painted Parrot: they could see the women walking up there.

Katie, Jill and Charlie arrived at the bar's outdoor tables just as the men did. Katie ran to Ford, gripping his shirt so tightly he was sure she'd pulled chest hairs right out. "Two hours and nothing, and now we get a no signal on the phones." Her voice was frantic, her hair blowing about her face, breaking free from her ponytail. Ford took both her hands in his and walked her backwards to the table where Gabe had just pulled out a chair to gently push his own wife into.

"Deep breaths and start from the beginning." Gabe pulled up a chair and sat, his knees touching Charlie's, his smile encouraging even as worry was building fast. Rory'd never been out of contact for long since she'd come to live with him on the island.

Nash and Jill stood arm in arm beside them while Ford leaned on a tree, his arm around Katie, stroking her arm gently.

"They've missed demands to check in, you know they never do that. We dismissed the first one because Katie said Owen had just run past the bakery shortly before. But then when they didn't check in the second time, we all compared notes and realized we hadn't heard a peep in over an hour—phone or walkie." Charlie pushed back her hair and sat back in the chair. The women had handled their concerns up until now, but with no contact, they'd called in backup.

"We left the little ones with Reggie and did a walkabout over the usual places, nothing," Jill spoke up.

"I called Luke so he could keep an eye out for them," Katie added.

"I've not had any luck, either." Luke strode up to the group, Tag at his side.

"I'm going to be sure Matteo and Jane can cover things, then let's talk about where we've looked and where to look again." Gabe went inside the bar, worry creasing his face once he was turned away from the group.

Since she'd come to the island to live with him, Rory had gone from clingy to free spirited, running amok about the island in safety. She'd never failed to check in with him or Charlie often and had absolutely never missed responding to their calls or texts. Ignoring the chill that prickled along his neck, Gabe ensured Matteo and Jane could call in their backup staff and run things as he and Nash had intended to be behind the bar this afternoon.

In minutes, a plan was made, and volunteers had joined in. Word spread quickly, and shop owners all promised to keep an eye out for the kids or any news to pass along. The groups scattered to their search areas, armed with first aid kits and walkie talkies as well as their phones.

Riding with Ford in the Jeep to check out Amos's area, Katie clutched her stomach, the knot inside cold and shaky.

"Thank you," she said over the noise of the wind.

"For what?" Ford shot her a quizzical expression.

"For not giving me a hard time about the freedom the kids have here. I know it makes you unsettled that they run amok like they do."

"It's a brave new world here. I'm glad they have it, you chose well. I'll adjust." Ford kept his eyes on the road, muscle in his jaw jumping.

Katie knew that was a big deal for him. Ford had grown up in less admirable areas of Chicago and had been disturbed to find she lived alone and went anywhere at any time of day or night without much thought for safety. Her neighborhood had been a little run down, but safety hadn't concerned Katie—likely because she had no choice but to rely on only herself. It had taken her some time to see Ford's concerns as care for her and not overprotective bullying. To his credit, in his time on the island, he'd only shown her his discomfort with the lack of direct supervision on the kids one time. Once he'd seen that the kids were savvy and safe with plenty of familiar adults within reach if needed, he'd worked hard to come to terms with their freedom.

Both scanned the hills on the way inland to Amos's place, but knew that Phil would scan the area from the helo and let them know if he saw anything. They were mostly concerned with Amos's property and the area adjacent to it. The kids roamed there often but usually got a ride as it was quite a ways from town into the hills.

Pulling up to Amos's house, Ford hopped out of the Jeep, Katie close behind him. "I'll go down by the dock and around by the campsite we found. Why don't you check the house and the animal areas?"

Katie nodded, already headed for the house, calling for the kids. "Miri? Owen, are you here? Rory?"

Ford kept his eyes on the ground around him as he walked the boardwalk out to Amos's fishing spot. The chairs remained as usual, an empty cooler stood open. He rubbed his forehead with his forefinger and thumb, looking out over the water. "Kids! Owen? Girls?" He called out, ignoring the tiny frisson of alarm crawling up his spine.

Seeing nothing out of the ordinary and hearing no answers to his calls, Ford walked into the woods, stepping quietly as he approached the drifter campsite they'd found several days ago. He was convinced both campsites they'd discovered belonged to the same person. That could be good or bad, depending on how you looked at it.

The campsite that had been tidy and secured the last time he'd been here was set up with a fire ring of rocks and a tipped-over small folding chair, a box of provisions next to it. The ashes were cold, but Ford felt like the place was inhabited; the air was disturbed here somehow—and recently. Something jiggled at the edges of his memory as he looked over the campsite, something vague yet familiar, but nothing popped to mind.

Ford ventured further into the woods, grateful to be out of the direct sunlight as his head was being contrary, messing around with his vision just enough to piss him off. Just before he turned around to retrace his steps, his walkie talkie crackled to life. Phil gave him the coordinates just to his east where he thought he'd seen bright yellow flash, which described Owen's shirt of the day. Ford responded and headed quickly in that direction.

Ford covered ground quickly, calling out as he went. "Owen! Miri! Rory!" He wanted the kids to hear him, drifter or no drifter.

His blood turned to ice as the air was split by a child's terrified shriek followed by sobs and cries of pain. "Miriam!" he bellowed, sliding down the rocky hill above a ravine, right about where Phil had advised him to look.

"Dad! Dad, she's going to fall again!" Owen yelled, seeing his father come down the hill to the ledge above the ravine. His terrified face was streaked with dirt, his hair matted with sweat and grime.

Ford clutched the boy to him when Owen grabbed him around the waist, his face pressed against Ford's side. "Hey, hey, just show me and let's help her." Ford bent to look into his son's face. Owen nodded, his eyes huge in his face as he pointed down the ravine.

"Rory slipped and fell a long time ago and we've been trying to get her out, but she's sleepy now. Miriam said she could climb down and help her, but she fell too. Dad, I was waiting and waiting for you—I tried to call over and over. I couldn't leave them and go back to Papa's where the signal is." Owen's words tumbled together in half sobs as his relief at being found overtook him.

"Okay, run back up until you have a signal and radio Gabe, then call Mom, okay?" Ford squeezed the boy's shoulder, handing him the phone and the walkie talkie along with his pack. "There's water, drink it."

Ford edged to the ravine's ledge, calling down. "Miriam? Miri, honey, talk to me. Rory?" He lay on the ground and scooted as close to the edge as he dared, hanging his head over the edge.

"Jesus," he breathed, his eyes closing for a moment as he struggled for control. All he wanted to do was jump down that wall and grab up those two little girls from the rocks. "Okay, overreacting isn't going to help them, Ace," he muttered, scooting out a little further. "Miri?"

This time her small voice piped up. "Daddy? Daddy, help!"

He could see her about twenty feet down, Rory curled up in a ball a few more feet down. "Miriam, listen to me, baby. Are you listening?"

"Daddy, Daddy, I'm going to fall again!" Miri's frantic voice rose on a scream.

"Miriam Elizabeth Callahan, listen to me." Ford raised his voice, calm, yet firm and loud enough to penetrate her hysteria. "Sit very still, okay, baby? Rory? Rory, darling, wake up and talk to me." Rory's lack of movement was of great concern, considering how far she'd fallen.

"She won't, Daddy," Miri said. "She was talking to us and said she was tired and went to sleep."

Ford hoped that news meant Rory was just exhausted and not suffering from a head injury or worse.

"Everyone is on their way, Dad." Owen came to Ford's side, breathing hard.

"Good job, son."

"Daddy!" Miri screamed, clearly hysterical and losing it fast. "Daddy, I'm falling!"

"Miriam, be still!" Ford bellowed, already sitting up and sliding his legs over the wall. He had to get down there and keep her from falling to her death, as the bottom of the ravine was still several hundred feet below Rory and filled with sharp rocks and branches.

"Dad!" Owen grabbed his arm, sending Ford into a slide he narrowly stopped with one hand wrapped around a low hanging tree branch.

"Owen." Ford gasped for breath. "Owen, I need you to go up there and watch for the others. Your mother will be here shortly, she's not far."

The boy nodded, scampering away from the edge to do his father's bidding.

Breathing a short-lived sigh of relief, Ford took a deep breath and let himself slide slowly. His admittedly futile hope was that his size would slow the slide and let him land near Miri without more than a sprained ankle or elbow.

"Miriam, honey, Daddy's coming down. I want you to scoot as far back against the wall as you can. Make yourself a tiny ball, okay?" The girl's racking sobs pierced his skull as he shook his head, trying to clear his vision.

It wasn't bad enough to take him out, at least he didn't think so. That was his last coherent thought as his vision went gray, Miri's screams echoing in his head.

*　*　*

He fought the instinct to push at whatever was choking him, forcing himself to calm down and assess the situation. First, he needed to breathe.

"Daddy! Daddy!" Ford now realized it was Miri's arms locked about his throat, her little tear-soaked face pressed against his. He struggled to relax and bring a hand up, finding his body uncooperative at the moment.

A hand came between Miri's death grip and his throat, gently easing her hold and letting him suck in blessed air.

"See, he's okay, look." The voice came from above Ford's head, out of his line of sight—not that his eyes would do him the favor of opening at the moment. His mind scrambled to place the familiar, yet out of place, voice.

Ford focused on breathing and letting his body wake up. His first reaction was to protect the girls from whoever this was, but the voice was so familiar he'd relaxed almost immediately. That puzzled him, or it would if he could get a coherent thought together.

"What's your name, honey?" The hand stayed at his throat, holding Miri's arms out just enough.

"M-Miri." The little girl's sobs had slowed to hiccups, her body still plastered to her father's chest.

"And your friend?"

"I'm Rory." A wave of relief flooded through Ford at hearing the other child's voice. He'd had no idea how badly she might be hurt when he'd seen her curled on the rocks below, unresponsive.

"Miri and Rory. Sounds like a TV show." The voice chuckled, the hand moving away now that Miri had let her grip ease. "Miri, I have some Gatorade right over there—see the gray box? Why don't you go get some for Rory and your dad?

Ford groaned, finally moving his head to find it still attached though pain shot through it and seemingly down his entire right side.

"Take it easy. The kids are banged up but gonna be okay. Unless I miss my guess, the cavalry will be here in minutes." A hand patted his shoulder before moving to his leg, which he now realized was throbbing and felt on fire.

Ford groaned again, this time managing to open his eyes and see the man helping them.

"Holy Mary, Mother of God, you?" he breathed, scrambling to sit upright.

CHAPTER FORTY-FIVE

THIS KEELING OVER and waking up somewhere else was really getting old, Ford grumbled to himself. Eyes still closed, he smelled the far too familiar hospital smells and heard monitor beeps and voices around him. With a bracing breath, he took stock of how he felt before opening his eyes. He'd learned to do that after he'd gotten blown up. Taking a moment before opening his eyes gave him a little time before people jumped to tend or talk to him.

"Ford?" Her hand came to rest on his arm, fingers stroking.

Ah, Katie. She was always so tuned in to him. He felt the first real twinge of regret that he'd shut her out during his recuperation and rehabilitation. He'd apologized already, repeatedly, but in his heart he'd still felt the decision had been the right one—until now.

Ford opened his eyes, blinking away the blurriness. "Katiebean." His throat felt like road rash, his voice gravelly. "Kids?"

"All going to be just fine. Miri sprained her wrist, Rory broke her leg, Owen is okay—cuts and bruises all around," Jill said, stepping up to Katie's side. "They're all with Gabe and Charlie in Rory's room, she's staying the night."

Ford breathed a sigh of relief, the panic easing. He pushed to sit up only to be restrained at his other shoulder by Nash's hand.

Katie pushed the button on the bed to help him, shoving another pillow behind his head. She was well aware of his aversion to lying flat.

"The man that helped us—where is he?" Ford was relieved to find his head tender, yet pain free, everything else as expected, barring snowy white bandages covering his right leg from hip to knee and an ice pack on his right wrist. He figured meds were to blame for the pain free part, but he'd take it for the moment.

"He disappeared into the woods as soon as Gabe found you. We've had a search team out, no luck," Nash replied.

"Call off the search," Ford said.

"But what if he was after the kids?" Nash objected. "We at least need to know who he is and why he's out there."

Ford shook his head, astonished that the room didn't spin. "Call. It. Off." He gave weight to each word.

"I did, Ford. Mostly." Luke stepped into the curtained cubicle. "While we all have questions for him, I saw no criminal evidence to waste manpower on a search. I'm keeping a deputy out there looking, because we do need to be sure." Luke shook Ford's good hand. "Looking good. I'd like to hear the whole story from you. I'll come by later."

"He's not a criminal, trust me on that. Take it easy during the search, okay?" At the moment, all Ford wanted was to escape this place, the oxygen shrinking in the room as he sat there. But he owed it to the man they were looking for to help as best he could. With that, he looked at Luke, "We can talk now, if it'd be easier."

Being good at his job meant Luke was well capable of reading between the lines when need be. Nodding, he gestured to the door. "Let me speak to Ford alone, please?"

Nash frowned but followed Jill while Katie stopped to kiss Ford's forehead, her brow furrowed as well.

A few minutes later, Luke left the cubicle with a wave to the trio waiting down the hall. "Talk to all of you soon," he called, making a quick exit, his phone already in hand.

They all went back to Ford, who was sitting on the edge of the bed, the sheet pooled in his lap. "Let's get out of here," he said, looking around for his clothes.

"The doctor has to release you, Ford. We need to be sure you're okay." Katie fixed him with a glare. "Humor me, for once, Ace."

Ford rolled his eyes. "The head was the usual, the leg caught a branch on the way down, the wrist got tweaked when I tried to hold my weight as long as possible. I'm good."

"You are good." Dr. Talbot pushed back the curtain with a smile. "Take care of those stitches, rest your wrist a few days and continue with your post-concussive care."

"The migraine triggers?" Katie asked, looking from Ford to the doctor.

"As soon as I start getting better sleep, they'll settle back down. It'll take time," Ford replied.

Dr. Talbot nodded. "He knows what to do."

"That's it?" Katie frowned.

The doctor nodded again and left the cubicle.

Nash clapped Ford's shoulder. "Glad to see your eyes, Ace. We'll check in later. We need to talk."

"Thanks, both of you." Ford returned Jill's hand squeeze. As their friends left the cubicle, he looked to Katie, knowing she'd have questions.

*   *   *

After hugs all around, Katie stood at the window while Nash and Jill said their goodbyes to Ford. She gazed out at the bustle of the bigger town across the channel from their small island, the edge of the sea barely visible off in the distance. Her stillness belied the churning of her thoughts.

Just as she'd thought she couldn't take any more after Ford, the baby, and now Amos's issues, the kids got hurt and Ford had lain there on the ground so still and pale—again. It seemed her world was always imploding into uncertainty and fear just as she got her feet under her. Hugging herself tightly, Katie mulled over the thought that had been slowly taking root in the back of her mind. Maybe hoping and waiting for things to settle into a groove wasn't what it was all about. After all the loneliness and uncertainty of growing up alone followed by the ever-present fear of the unknown when Ford was deployed all those years, maybe life overall was never on an even keel. But maybe, in spite of the unknowns, it was always filled with hope and love if you chose to see it. Maybe the key wasn't to find a calm in which to weigh anchor, but to learn to ride the waves together, to grab on to each other and hang on tight. Granted, the two of them had sucked at that eight months ago, but did those mistakes—those massive, horrible mistakes—nullify all that had come before and since, or all that could be?

With those thoughts tumbling about in her head, Katie turned to find Ford dressed and ready to go.

"We'll talk on the way?" Ford reached out for her hand.

Gratified that Ford acknowledged he had some explaining to do after effectively shooing her out while he talked to Luke, Katie took his hand so they could leave the hospital behind.

CHAPTER FORTY-SIX

"ARE YOU TRYING TO KILL ME, or worse, maim me badly so I'm an invalid for the rest of my life?" Nash jumped out of the way of falling lumber just in the nick of time.

"Sorry!" Ford's voice came from the tree limbs. Mostly hidden from sight by the leaves, only Ford's legs were visible, with Owen's feet and Gabe's legs sticking out from up there too.

"He thought I had it and I thought he had it." Gabe's muffled voice held suppressed laughter.

"Sure as hell won't be funny when you have to help my wife push my wheelchair or wipe my ass," Nash bellowed back, picking up the lumber pieces one by one and feeding them back up into hands that appeared out of the tree leaves.

"Be sure to kill him, not maim him 'cause I sure don't want to wipe his ass," Owen said matter of factly.

All three men laughed, the tree climbers nailing down the last three boards before climbing down the sturdy, wide ladder.

"Just the railing left to finish." Ford headed for the backyard grill he rarely got a chance to use, as they were at the beach or the bar much of the time. Today they'd chosen to gather in the back yard.

Katie and Jill brought out fruit platters and the meat for the grill, Charlie following with a big salad and a tray of Katie's tarts. Rory was settled with pillows in a lounge chair, her right leg in a bright green cast with Miri similarly snuggled in another chair next to her, her wrist bound in a pink elastic bandage. Scarlett was cheerfully waiting on the girls hand and foot, complete with a little tray and apron as she fetched drinks and snacks and coloring books.

"Rory seem okay to you?" Katie murmured to Charlie, just out of the girls' earshot.

"A little quiet but generally herself as she is when she's a little sick, maybe. Why? Miri okay?" Charlie watched both girls color quietly.

Katie sighed. "You know how Miri has been with her anxiety. I expected it to be worse after witnessing her Daddy go down in front of her and a stranger coming out of nowhere to help them. But I don't know for sure what to do about it."

Jill joined them, Zane asleep in his playpen. "I noticed Miri hasn't said much the last couple times I've seen her."

"She will not let Ford out of her sight for one second—-not even to let him pee in peace."

Charlie settled into a chair, the others doing the same in a semicircle. Pushing back her windblown curls, she kept her voice low. "When Rory first came to Gabe, after her mother died, she didn't say much at all, and she was never far from his side. She'd seem fine but would suddenly drop what she was doing to run and find him. At first she cried for her mother, then she'd just cling to him. Their first days together were spent at Gabe's childhood home with his parents. Gabe said his mother told him to just be there for her, hold her when she came to him and just take it as it comes. It seems to have worked. She started playing longer and longer without running to his side, and eventually the sadness passed for the most part."

"So you think it's fine to just let it ride for now? She has brought up the stranger a few times, talked to Ford about it, so it's not like she's not talking about it at all." Katie chewed her bottom lip, her eyes going from her quiet girl to Ford at the grill. Laughing at something Nash said, he looked healthy and strong despite the glaring bandage on his leg. She made a face; after treehouse building, it sure wasn't a white bandage anymore.

"I think so, we all know to watch out for her. It might just take some time to find a groove again, you know?" Jill put in.

Katie nodded, smiling as Scarlett brought her a sticky cup of lemonade, the little girl grinning widely. "Thank you, darling girl."

"I'm starving, let's get that meat done, boys!" Jill called, mock swooning in hunger.

"Don't worry, honey, I'm on it!" Nash returned, turning to show her a platter filled with meat fresh off the grill.

"My hero!" she laughed as they all moved towards the table.

* * *

"Sunset!" Owen yelled, the puppy plus Rory's dog, Jake, barking and running in circles around him as he ran for the back gate with Scarlett on his heels. Jill and Nash followed, Zane riding tall on his father's shoulders.

Gabe bent in front of Rory's chair and scooped her into his arms. "Your chariot, m'lady."

Rory giggled, settling comfortably against him. Charlie draped a beach towel over the girl, as the evening air could be a little cool if you were sitting around.

Ford knelt in front of Miri's chair where she sat on the edge, wide eyed and silent. "Want a piggyback ride?" he asked with a conspiratorial wink.

The little girl nodded, a ghost of a smile crossing her face. Katie brought up the rear of the posse, latching the gate behind her.

In minutes, the motley crew was scattered on the sand with others, kids and dogs running amok, Rory sitting on Charlie's lap while Miri sat on Katie's.

Gabe strolled up to Ford where he stood, hands in his pockets, gazing out to sea.

Glancing about to ensure they were alone, he spoke quietly. "Miri okay?"

Ford shrugged. "I have no fucking idea." Realizing how harshly he'd spoken, Ford looked at Gabe, his mouth twisting wryly. "Sorry."

Gabe held up a hand. "Not necessary, I get it."

"Feeling helpless after what happened on the ridge is one thing, but, Gabe, I'm damn near useless to them. Why am I still around? Don't take this the wrong way, but what good am I serving them being here if I pass out every time I'm needed, if my daughter is terrified I'm going to be hurt at any moment? If my wife couldn't share her deepest sorrow with me? Let's keep going back to eight months ago when I royally fucked up and started this domino shitstorm." The torrent of words just wouldn't stop.

Gabe looked over to Nash, who took his cue and handed the baby to Jill with a word in her ear. Jill turned to join Katie and

Charlie on the beach blanket where they carefully kept the sand from Rory's cast.

"Come with us." Nash tugged Ford's arm as Gabe headed up the beach towards his cottage and the woodshop where he'd lived in the back room before Charlie had come along.

"Miri will freak out," Ford hesitated, catching Katie's eye when she turned to look at him.

Katie gave him a slight smile and a nod. They'd come find him if they needed him.

*   *   *

Ford had been in the woodshop before, seeking out Gabe for one reason or another, but he'd not noticed the huge punching bag hanging in the back corner.

"Ford, meet Big Al. He's either your best friend or your ass kicker, depending." Nash swung the black bag at Ford, catching him squarely in the chest.

"Oof."

"You want gloves or you brave enough to tape only?" Gabe held up said items.

"Tape. Gloves are for wimps." Ford grinned.

Gabe set about taping Ford's hands while Nash rummaged around the fridge for beer. "Probably shouldn't do this with that wrist—go easy on it, okay?"

Ford nodded, flexing his fingers in the extra tight tape job.

"So you think living at the B&B and staying away from Katie and the kids is best for them?" Gabe eyed the other man critically.

"I do, although I haven't been there much with all that's been going on." Ford nodded, flexing his fingers, testing the tape. When it was done, Nash gave Big Al a shove at him again, standing clear.

"You think leaving your wife is helping her?" Gabe leaned against the woodworking table where tools and charity toys were in various stages of progress.

"She told me it's what she wants, repeatedly." Ford gave Big Al an experimental punch, the jolt of pleasurable pain, yet not pain, shooting up his arm.

"Have you not been at her side since you got home? Helping with the kids, the bakery, Amos?" Nash chimed in, following Gabe's lead.

"I have. And every damn time, either I pass out like a candy ass or she doesn't want my help." Ford began a series of punches, punctuating his words. He punched hard with his left hand, less so with his weakened right one.

"So you didn't help save the kids and get them safe?" Gabe sipped his beer idly.

"I did not. Phil found them, all I did was terrify my daughter by passing out in front of her, topped off by bringing a stranger to her rescue," Ford grunted, his punches faster and harder.

Nash grinned at Gabe. Big Al therapy worked every time, even drunk. Gabe could attest to that as, before Rory had come into his life, he could often be found flat out on the floor under Big Al, having lost to Johnny Walker Blue Label and the badass punching bag time and again on sleepless nights. His need for those rounds had disappeared after Rory and Charlie had settled in on the island, Rory adjusting and Charlie eventually marrying him.

"And what about her keeping the baby from me? *A baby.*" Ford grunted again, his punches stinging his taped hands. That took the wind out of his sails and Ford slid down the wall with a whoosh. "A baby," he whispered, dropping his head into his hands. "He would have fit in my hand." Ford pulled back a hand, opening and closing it.

"No more trying to live around the elephants in the room, Ace." Gabe reached down to pull the other man up, pulling him into a brief, hard hug. "Let us take the kids with us, go home and hash this out, fight, grieve, something."

Ford nodded wearily.

"In fact, go home and shower. We'll send her." Nash gave Ford's sweaty shoulder a shove.

"Thanks." Ford waved a taped, battered hand and jogged out the door.

CHAPTER FORTY-SEVEN

HAVING BEEN PUSHED off the beach by their friends, Katie walked up to the porch where Ford sat on the steps in the moonlight. She sat down beside him, close enough for their bodies to touch. "I need to say I'm sorry. I'm sorry for believing the worst of you when I should have trusted you, in spite of how hurt I was to be shut out. I should have acknowledged you probably weren't thinking straight—ya know, concussion and all-I should have given you a chance to explain when you were ready. Add that to my own is-issues, then I have to share a majority of the blame for failing us." With that, she let out a huge sigh, as if the words had taken the energy out of her.

Bolstered by her words and the fact that she'd sat down so close to him, Ford reached over and took her hand. Gazing out into the dark, he took a few more deep, fortifying breaths.

"I need to say I'm sorry, too," he began.

Katie shook her head, "You already did that, several times."

"Hear me out." He jiggled their joined hands, his thumb rubbing hers.

"While I believed what I did in those first days after was the right thing to do for you, for us, I admit I was wrong. I should have trusted that you could have handled it beside me. I should have trusted in us."

Katie leaned her head against his shoulder. "I think we've said all we need to say about that part of things, don't you? But now that you know the secret I didn't mean to keep, we have that to deal with."

Ford grimaced at that. "The baby..." He let his words trail off—he was doing that a lot lately it seemed.

"It's tough for you when you can't fix it, Ace. You've spent your life fixing problems one after the other, including mine—maybe even especially mine. I know that. But no more running to spare me pain—that doesn't work. Stop doing what doesn't work. You know that's—"

Ford interrupted, "The definition of insanity, I know, I know."

"Can you forgive me?" she whispered.

"Can you count on me? Believe I'm here to stay?" Ford looped his arms around her waist, letting his head fall forward.

Cupping his face in her hands, she urged him to look up at her. "I do believe that." She kissed the scar at his forehead, kissed both his closed eyes and leaned into him, resting her head against his. Ford shifted to sit up fully, drawing her onto his knee. He kissed just below her ear and followed her jawline to her lips, dropping tiny, feathery kisses all the way before he covered her mouth with his.

They sighed into the deep, slow kiss. This time was different. There were no more buts, no more if onlys, no more secrets holding a cold space in her heart. Ending the kiss with her head resting against his heart, they sat simply holding space together.

If he could only forgive her, if she could only trust him, this could be a new beginning, right here on the porch with everyone and everything they loved close by.

While he held her in this moment, breathing in her familiar lavender and coffee scent, Ford realized that even if she had told him about Orion before, it wouldn't have changed anything. He couldn't have been there to hold both of them during his son's fleeting moments on earth. At that time, he'd been out of his mind, his broken body racked with devastating pain. So while, yes, she should have told him much sooner, who was he to dictate how she'd chosen to handle it after his own wrecked decisions?

His heartbeat quickened to think that they just might have tumbled together over the last big hurdle.

* * *

Going on a strong hunch that kept niggling in the back of his mind, Ford slipped away to Amos's dock for a little while one afternoon.

With Amos still in the hospital, the place was deserted and still except for the animals Keno had been tending to for the old man.

Ford sat down in Amos's favorite chair, just inches from the calm water of the inlet, popped open one of the six pack he'd brought and waited.

He didn't have long to wait. The man dressed in camo pants and a brown t-shirt dropped into the chair next to him within minutes.

"Thanks for being there for me and the kids, Trevor," Ford said, without looking at him.

"Right place, right time." The other man shrugged, reaching down to take a beer from the six pack.

Ford then turned his head to look at his fellow medic, his right-hand man, his friend. "Trevor, it's never been about right place, right time. You're a hero, plain and simple."

Trevor's face was gaunt, his eyes shadowed. "You nearly died. The rest of them did die. Not sure how that makes me a hero."

"What makes you a hero is showing up, giving your all. Every time. For me, for the others, for my kids you helped the other day. For your wife, Trevor."

Trevor drained the beer, dropping the bottle to the sand and leaning forward to rest his elbows on his knees. Chin in hands, he cleared his throat a few times. "I failed you, I failed our men and I failed Jackie."

"How could you have failed me—I'm alive. And well, I might add. The kids are safe and whole. The others? We all know the risks, Trevor. We've done this for far too long not to." Ford reached over to grip Trevor's arm. "As for Jackie, let her come take you home. She misses you."

"I'm not sure I can do that. What about the nightmares? The flashbacks? How can we find normal after all we've seen and done, Ford?" Trevor's voice was tortured. He scrubbed his hands over his eyes, leaving them there.

"She'll get you some help, real help that will make a difference. Trust me when I say the love of a good woman, one that's willing to stick with you, makes all the difference. While normal might not happen, a new groove can." Ford willed Trevor to hear his words, really hear them.

PTSD was no light matter, not even on a good day. Trevor had been dealing with his alone for nearly three months, since he'd gone missing from home. His wife had called Ford to let him know Trevor was gone, but Ford had never dreamed Trevor had seen the group emails and followed his friend to where he was now. The soldier had been living in the woods, apparently befriending Amos along the way.

Now, Trevor nodded at Ford's words, reaching over to grip Ford's hand where it still gripped his arm. "I'm so tired, man. So fucking tired."

"I know, Trev. Believe me, I know." Ford held the other man's gaze. "Come with me, we'll get Jackie here."

After texting Gabe for backup, Ford took Trevor to his room at the B&B, watching him carefully along the way to ensure he was okay in town, around other people. Trevor seemed to be exhausted, letting himself be led almost like a child. Once inside the room, Ford steered Trevor to the shower while he answered Gabe's knock on the door.

Gabe had brought food and drinks as requested. This would let Ford keep Trevor in the room until Jackie arrived. He knew Trevor had reached the end of his rope. Best-case scenario meant he'd crash and sleep, knowing he was in safe hands. Worst case—well, Ford didn't intend to think about worst case until he had to.

"I can't believe he just walked up and sat down to talk to you." Gabe shook his head incredulously. "After running alone for so long."

"You know how deep a bond can go when you're in charge of each other's lives," Ford said. "I'm just glad it went down without incident. Now I just keep him calm until tomorrow afternoon, and he'll be on his way with Jackie to find his way back to real life."

"You want me to stay, just in case?" Gabe asked, putting the drinks and pie slices in the room's small fridge.

"No, I think he'll settle and sleep if it's just me here. I'll yell if need be," Ford replied.

With that, Gabe left before Trevor stepped out of the bathroom, clad in a pair of Ford's shorts.

Ford made the necessary phone calls to get Trevor's wife there as quickly as possible, skipping commercial flights by calling on friends with medical and flying connections.

Taking in the other man's glazed eyes, Ford simply tucked him into the bed where Trevor was asleep in seconds.

Ford settled into the recliner with his supper, the television on mute, and called Katie. She'd be relieved Trevor was no longer at large, so to speak.

Ford himself was glad to know for sure the stranger wasn't a stranger after all, and that Trevor was safe and soon to be getting the help he needed.

It felt good to take care of those in his life again. Really good.

CHAPTER FORTY-EIGHT

GOT A FEW MINUTES to pop by the house?

The text came up on Katie's phone just as she dried her hands and turned to the icing table.

Sure.

She texted Ford back and called to Reggie at the front of the store, "Be back in a few, nothing needs watching back here."

"Got it, Bosslady!" Reggie called back, refilling the cookie display while Matteo leaned idly on the counter, shamelessly flirting with her.

Puzzled, Katie called out as she stepped inside the house next door, "Ford? Everything okay?"

"That depends." He walked in the back door, using his shirt to wipe sweat from his face and bare torso.

"Depends?" she echoed, her mouth going dry at the sight of him, heat flooding through her. Since their heart and soul reunion on the beach a few days ago, her body felt tingly and alive, tender and on fire—especially to look at him looking at her like he was now.

"It depends," he weighed each word carefully, "on what you think of booty calls." With a low chuckle, he crossed the room and pulled her close, her knees going weak as he took her mouth straight into a deep, hard kiss.

"Booty calls?" she croaked, the tangy scent of clean sweat combined coupled with his mouth's shenanigans making her head spin.

"Shower booty calls to be exact." Ford walked her backwards down the hall, his arms keeping her steady, his damp hair brushing her chin as he licked and nipped along her jaw.

"Sh—shower?" Katie gave up trying to hold on to any coherent thought and let her head fall forward against the top of his. They reached the bathroom where he reached around the tiled half wall into the shower to turn on the water, then pressed her to the wall, his arms braced on either side. One of Katie's favorite things about this island house was the spacious walk-in shower, complete with a bench along the wall.

"I know you've had shower booty calls before—I was witness and cheerful participant to every one." He didn't waste any time in stripping off her t-shirt, dropping to one knee to unbutton and tug off her shorts. His hair brushed her bare legs as he pressed kisses to her knee and dragged his mouth slowly up her inner thigh before standing slowly drawing his body up hers, skin to skin. He backed into the steam-filled shower, taking her with him. Once under the warm rain spray, his eyes on hers, he turned her around. Placing each of her hands on the wall, his own hands slowly followed the path of the water sluicing down her arms, down her back. Wordlessly, he pressed himself to her, his groan deep, heartfelt. Her answering sound was barely a whimper as a hand caressed its way down her back slowly, slipping between her legs. Dropping his head to her shoulder, his other hand swept the dark mahogany slick of her wet hair to the side so he could plant tiny kisses all along her neck, sliding down further with each kiss.

Later, nestled between his legs on the shower bench, she held up a finger. "I'm a fan."

"Hmm?" Ford's voice rumbled against her back, his ragged breath slowing.

"You asked me what I thought of booty calls."

Ford's laugh echoed off the shower walls, his arms squeezing her tight.

CHAPTER FORTY-NINE

KATIE'S ARRIVAL EIGHT MONTHS AGO had been a renewal in the old man's life; Amos hadn't felt so alive since his beloved Bessie had died seven years before. Suddenly he'd noticed the sun was brighter, the fish biting more, the food tasting wonderful. While he loved his friends and Gabe did his damnedest to be the son Amos had never had, there was nothing like the love of family—especially a girl like Katie, who knew what it was to be alone in the world. She'd thrown her heart and soul into loving him and reestablishing her grandmother's bakery, making a good life for her family here on the island. She had a good man, too, if she'd accept that his flaws made him strive to be a better man.

Katie and her man had just left him, promising they'd be taking him home. Home to his house, to his fishing dock, to his Bessie. They'd talked to him about his health issues, about how it would make life easier if he didn't live alone anymore. Surprisingly them both, Amos had agreed. He'd told Katie he wanted life to be good for her, for the kids, not to be bothering with an old man who talked to a ghost. Katie and Ford both had protested soundly, telling Amos he was to remain, always, in the center of their world.

Even though some—okay many—days he could feel the edges of his memory blur as he'd look for his glasses over and over or blank on the fishing lure he wanted to use, Amos was certain life would go good for a while longer—maybe a medicine or two to bother with—but he had family, his fishing dock and Bessie. Nodding to himself, Amos dozed off in the chair.

* * *

This is what ten years of marriage has come to, Ford thought as he took a deep breath of fresh air upon stepping out of the hospital. If holding hands in a hospital elevator after seeing a beloved old man they planned to care for together—while her phone buzzed with texts from friends who were caring for their children and his radio crackled low with dispatch chatter—didn't epitomize a ten year marriage, he didn't know what did.

Wind blowing through the Jeep, the sun warm and strong, they rode across the island without talking, the weight of the day melting away.

Katie's head was back against the seat, her shades on, feet on the dash as Bon Jovi's 'Livin' on a Prayer' spilled from the speakers out into the island air. Ford drove with the wind in his hair, a hand on her knee, just being for a change.

"This is more like it!" Katie raised her voice above the music, a smile lighting her face.

"In a hurry?" he called, a wicked grin spreading across his face.

She shook her head. "The kids are with Charlie, happy as clams."

With a wink, Ford pulled into a deli just before the road crossed over the bay. He pointed at Katie and held up one finger. He returned shortly with a full bag, reaching into one and handing her a bottle of ice cold local-made lemonade.

Clinking their bottles together, he drove out of town. Her hand rested on his thigh, her fingers making distracting little circles as she tapped her foot to the music and gazed out at the sea below the road.

Minutes later, Ford parked the Jeep, gathered up the bags and jumped out. He rummaged around in the back of the Jeep, tossing her a folded blanket.

Katie followed him, climbing up the rocky path behind him, stepping through a break in the rocks. She paused at the beauty of the quiet cove in front of her. The circle of rocks protected the small stretch of beach from the wind, and the sand was smoothed by the sea, the only marks being the prints of birds and crabs.

Just out of the tide's reach, Ford set the bags down and spread out the blanket. With a bow and a gallant wave of both arms, he gestured to Katie. "Milady."

She smiled, kicking off her shoes and sitting in the middle of the blanket.

Joining her, Ford sat cross legged, pulling the bags to him. She needed to eat, and he intended to see that she did. He looked up to find her watching him, her eyes dark, expression soft. He leaned in for a light, soft kiss, holding a sandwich in each hand. Katie took the food from him and set it aside, scooting in close, deepening the kiss.

"Wait. I have something for you." He pushed up his shirt, pointing to a snug bandage over his heart. "You've yet to ask about this."

"You get bumps 'n' bruises all the time, I was rather preoccupied a few moments ago." She winked at him, drawing a finger across the bandage.

With a wince, Ford yanked the bandage free, revealing a tattoo, the ink so fresh the skin around it was still reddened.

Katie's hand flew to her mouth as the fingers of her other hand very lightly traced the shooting star about the size of two quarters side by side. Orion's name was delicately etched in blue along the star's trail. "Oh, Ford."

"It matches your pendant," he whispered, touching her necklace with a fingertip.

Katie leaned forward to gingerly kiss the tender tattooed skin. "I love you, Ace. Always have, always will."

"I love you, Bean. Always have, always will." He kissed her lips, then her cheek where a tear rolled down.

She pushed him back to lay on the blanket, sliding her body over his. Ford sure wasn't going to complain, no sir. Straddling him, she nudging him to lift up so she could pull off his t-shirt. She tossed it aside with a flourish and the sexiest smile he'd ever seen in his life. She then reached up and tugged the band free from her hair, letting it fall in a shiny chestnut wave over her shoulders so that it curtained around his face when she leaned over to kiss him again.

With a look that scorched him to the core, she sat back up and unbuttoned her shirt slowly. Leaving it hanging open, a bikini top visible, she brushed her fingers across his bare chest, teasing, finally leaning down to bring their bodies together.

Captivated by her, his chest on fire where her fingers brushed, Ford reached up to cup her face in his hands, the kiss igniting deep fires that had lain banked for far too long. Without the anger of the past year hanging between them, with the beginning of fresh healing after her secret's revelation, their tempo grew faster, the need to be fully together eclipsing all else.

Katie sat up, shrugging off her shirt, keeping her eyes on his as she tossed away the bikini top, too. With a growl, Ford wrapped his arms around her and rolled, making her laugh with his nuzzles to her neck before he sobered and kissed all along her collarbone. He scattered kisses across soft, slightly salty skin, whispering, "Mine," with every one.

Katie slid her arms around him, her fingers caressing every inch, the contours of his body so familiar, their legs tangled together. She wanted him touching every single part of her, head to toe. She wanted to cling to him, hold him tightly and never, ever let him go again.

As the sun set in its usual splendor, the vibrant colors crescendoing together then fading into the indigo and orange of tropical twilight, heated touches, deep moans and soft gasps drifted through the tiny cove as finally, finally at long last, the last of the shattered pieces of the the two of them fell into place.

Ford and Katie put each other back together again—piece by piece, kiss by kiss, moment by moment.

All was as it should be.

CHAPTER FIFTY

KATIE DEFTLY SHAPED the loaves of bread in the bakery's kitchen after hours, considering her visit to the hospital today. Amos was ready to come home—but to what home, and how would she care for him? The more she thought about it, the more she realized the only solution was for her to close the bakery and take care of Amos. It was what Amos deserved.

What better way to try and learn to trust Ford again, to build their future together, than to dive in headfirst with juggling family life? With Ford home to stay and her closing the bakery, they could go back and forth from their cottage to Amos's place. That would keep Amos in his groove and happy, and Ford would work his shifts, fish with Gabe and Nash, continue to find his place in island life. The kids, bless 'em, would keep on being awesome every day. All would be good, there would just be no bakery in the way of her priority—taking care of Amos and her family. Sliding the loaves into the proofer, her hands lingered on the door. She wouldn't waste time feeling sorry for herself—she knew better than most how futile that was—but it didn't hurt to give the bakery and the life it gave her a few moments of regret for dreams realized and let go.

* * *

Night on the beach was magical, as usual. Despite whatever might come about, Katie loved the fact that the island always came through with sunrise and sunset, tides would always ebb and flow. And every day, she'd find her friends here. She was learning to believe she'd find Ford here, as well as in many other moments of her day now. Sure enough, just as she stepped onto the sand, he was there waiting. Smiling, he held out a hand. "It's a crime to miss sunset on the island, you know."

"I had one last bread batch to squeeze in." She swallowed hard at the truth of her words, her fingers involuntarily squeezing his tightly.

"What is it, Bean?" He tipped her chin up so her eyes met his. The blue darkened as he held her gaze, letting her lose herself in him for a moment, his arms looping around her waist.

"I've figured out what to do about Amos." She brushed dark waves from his temple; tangling her fingers in his hair always soothed her somehow. In all his years with Army hair, she hadn't realized she missed the short waves until now. It really was the little things.

"Do tell."

Drawing a deep breath, she looked down the beach where their friends laughed and the kids frolicked about with the dogs, the twilight magical, the sea darkening yet sparkling under the brightening moon.

"I'm closing the bakery for good." Her voice was quiet but strong. She was resolute.

Ford drew back, one hand still at her hip.

"I can't take care of Amos and the kids and also run the bakery, not the way I want to." She looked back into his eyes. "And you. I want to learn to be there for you again."

Ford nodded. "I understand, but before you do that, will you hear me out?"

She gave him a puzzled look. "Okay." She'd expected more surprise and protest from him, somehow.

"Let's join them." Ford nudged her to walk with him.

"Wait, what is it you want to say?" Katie resisted his tug.

"Humor me." He tugged harder, chuckling as she stumbled and swore before she finally just walked along with him.

They joined the scattered circle of chairs and beach towels near the water's edge, Ford dropping into a chair and pulling her to sit on his knee. "What I have to say includes these people."

Katie raised an eyebrow and looked around at her friends, all of them now paying attention to Ford.

Jill sent her a reassuring smile while Charlie echoed it with a wink that told her they knew just what was going on.

"Katie has just told me she's closing the bakery soon," Ford said, holding up a hand when Jill protested, "What? Wait, did you—?"

"News to me," Reggie laughed, confusing Katie further, as she'd expected a much more emotional reaction from her friend and partner. Matteo lounged next to her, privately hoping he could later convince Reggie to call this a first date.

Puzzled, Katie looked to her husband, who winked, one hand settled at her hip, the other on her knee.

"Katie, we've been doing some talking about you." Gabe spoke up from his place near the fire, leaning up to sit on the edge of his seat.

Charlie nodded. "A lot of talking about you."

"Behind your back, too." Nash grinned, tickling the baby rolling about on the beach towel between Jill's legs.

Katie frowned and started to speak, but Gabe held up a hand. "All teasing aside, Katie," he turned to face her, his expression serious. "We've been talking about you, about Amos—we included Ford after we'd started the conversation. This is not Ford alone, but he did have a big part in it." Gabe didn't want Katie to turn on Ford and accuse him of taking over. Over the past eight months, he'd learned how important her independence was to her.

"We love you, we love the kids and you know how much we all love Amos," Charlie said, her smile warm and comforting.

Katie nodded, chewing her bottom lip.

This time it was Jill that spoke up. "I never thought about you closing the bakery, but I suppose I should have realized you would do anything to make things as perfect as possible for Amos."

Gabe stood up to add a couple of pieces of wood to the fire. Taking a folded paper from his pocket, he walked over and handed it to Katie. "This is a list of everyone who wants to help with Amos's care."

Katie unfolded the paper to see a list of least twenty names and numbers. Names of her friends, Amos's friends, some names she barely knew from the bakery, others she saw in town from time to time, some she didn't know at all.

"When we say help with Amos's care, I mean every single person on that list has said they want to be with him for a few hours every day. Obviously you don't need them all every day, but they're ready for you to make a schedule every week so Amos can stay home. Nobody was asked, they came to me, to Gabe, to Jill, to Nash, to Charlie. All because they want to help you help Amos," Ford told her, his thumb brushing away her tears as they fell.

"But everyone has their own life to tend to." Katie held up her open hands and let them fall, looking at the faces around the fire.

"And everyone wants Amos and your family in our lives. Every day." Luke joined the group, Jane at his side.

"Sorry we're late, we got held up," she said, smothering a grin when Luke shot her a look, stifling his own grin.

"You two." Katie laughed at their sheepish faces. "Finally."

"So no closing the bakery, no taking this on by yourself. I'm here. They're here." Ford's arm around her waist held her close. For her ears only he said, "You're not alone, Bean, never again."

"We're all here because we want to be here. Those other names on the list? They expect a call, they're waiting to know how they can help. You're one of us, Katie." Charlie got up, Katie meeting her in a hug.

Jill joined them as Nash opened a bakery box to rave over the food inside. "As if we'd let you stop doing this to us!" he moaned, biting into one of the new pretzel-covered, caramel-drizzled brownie bites.

The mood was light, the music drifted down from the bar, the stars sparkled in the sky.

"Look, Dad, Aquila!" Owen called from the edge of the sea where he was chasing and being chased by Scout and Jake.

The boys playing with him looked where he pointed. "What's Aquila?"

Ford gave the boy a thumbs up as Owen drew in the sky, explaining what they were looking at to his friends.

*   *   *

At the edge of the light, where the darkness gathered between the firelight and The Painted Parrot's glow, Katie sat between Ford's legs, both of them facing the sea. Miri slept on the blanket beside them, Scarlett talking to herself next to her sister.

"She's doing so much better just in the last few days," Katie murmured, brushing her daughter's temple lightly, marveling at her eyelashes, her smooth little girl cheeks.

"She found me earlier and told me my friend helped her." Ford covered the child with an edge of the blanket, his hand lingering on her shoulder. "She said when I was hurt, he told her about me, about the Army and what a good job we did making the world safer. He told her she shouldn't be afraid, that my body was healing from that hard work and that she could help by being strong."

"Incredible insight. We'll have to thank Trevor when we get a chance. How is he, have you heard?" Katie closed her eyes and let out a breath, relaxing into his arms.

"He's doing better. The first few days he was nearly catatonic, just really out of it. Then he started talking, they made a treatment plan and he'll be trying time at home soon," Ford replied, leaning his head back to look at the sky.

"The stars are so bright out here, almost as bright as they were in the Sandbox—without the scary environment." Ford shuddered for effect.

"The starlight has always been our anchor, our way to find each other. It's only fitting that we end up out here where it's so clear," Katie replied.

"Look." Ford pointed to a shooting star.

Katie also pointed just to the east of his finger. "Another one?"

"Nah, it was the same one—it just moved," Ford replied, laughing loudly enough to make a few heads turn briefly when Katie realized his joke and pinched his thigh, hard.

"Ouch," Ford grunted, tightening his arms slightly. In this moment, his heart so full it was a wonder it could still beat. His son talking stars with his friends, his girls asleep next to him—Scarlett's little bare foot hooked over his ankle, Miri snuggled close to his knee.

"I know it's been such a hard road, Bean. I'm so sorry for all the broken promises. I'll make new ones."

"You're not going to promise me the moon, now are you?" Katie elbowed him as the full moon shone in all its glory above them.

Ford's chuckle rumbled in his chest, tickling her back. "I think we're both far too realistic for that. But I can—and do—promise to be here, to do this together."

Katie pulled his arms tighter around her. "I promise the same. No more lone ranger, we're in this together."

Ford kissed her temple, leaving his lips there. "We're okay, Bean. We're all okay."

* * *

<center>~~~~~~~~~~~THE END~~~~~~~~~~~~~~</center>

If you liked Bridges of Starlight and want to read more about the island, the community and The Painted Parrot, you can find Gabe and Charlie's story, Shades of Blue, on Amazon.

*Visit Dana's website for all Dana-Related News.
http://danabritt.com

*Meet up with her on Facebook—she's quite chatty there.
https://www.facebook.com/dtbritt1?fref=ts&em=1

*Sign up for Dana's monthly newsletter—news plus fun stuff.
https://goo.gl/lDX871

ACKNOWLEDGMENTS

raises sweet tea glass

Always in Treasured Memory of my Mother, Charlotte Tanaro. The world is never quite right when your mother is gone from it...

Jay and Meghan, my All Grown Up Babies--my Hearts, walking around in the world being incredible.

My Great Big Menagerie of an Extended Family--the love we've been given from those who came before us is the fabric of all of our lives, and their legacy. We honor it by remembering and by loving each other. I love you all, every one.

My First Reader, your belief in me is humbling--or would be if I could possibly be a humble person! Love you more'n my luggage, Betty.

Madame Editor, Sophie Weeks, you help me make my stories the best they can possibly be in spite of my 'persistent rebellions'. I read once that a good editor is akin to a person who walks into a room, spies a little-noticed door in the corner and says, "What's in here?" That describes what you do for me quite well. Let's gear up for book three, shall we?

My Circle of Friends Facebook group, thank you all from the bottom of my heart for being friends, for having fun in our group and for being dedicated supporters and cheerleaders of my stories.

www.ingramcontent.com/pod-product-compliance
Lightning Source LLC
Chambersburg PA
CBHW060326260626
47160CB00007B/2690